BARONESS
OF THE
EASTERN SEABOARD

AMID THE VASTNESS
OF ALL ELSE SAGA
BOOK SIX

BARONESS
OF THE
EASTERN
SEABOARD

C.S. HUMBLE

SHORTWAVE
PUBLISHING

Cover and interior design by Alan Lastufka.

First Shortwave Edition published September 2025.

10 9 8 7 6 5 4 3 2 1

ISBN 978-1-959565-72-7 (Paperback)
ISBN 978-1-959565-73-4 (eBook)

Amid the Vastness of All Else Saga

That Light Sublime Trilogy

Book 1 – The Massacre at Yellow Hill

Book 2 – A Red Winter in the West

Book 3 – The Light of a Black Star

The Peregrine Estate Trilogy

Book 4 – To Carry a Body to Its Resting Place

Book 5 – San Antonio Mission

Book 6 – The Baroness of the Eastern Seaboard

For Rae Wilde

Our words hold power, they are the ink that shapes the world.

"Live to the point of tears."

ALBERT CAMUS, *THE STRANGER*

"So I go. I travel farther and faster and harder than most, and I read, and I write, and I love cities. To be alone in a crowd, apart and belonging, to have distance between what I see and what I am."

AMAL EL-MOHTAR & MAX GLADSTONE, *THIS IS HOW YOU LOSE THE TIME WAR*

PREFACE

Living within the world, at any given time, are twenty-five gunfighters legally authorized to enact contests (duels) within the lawful boarders of the United States of America.

These twenty-five artisans of the quickdraw, bound by the rules of their professional association, are numbered among the most dangerous soloist mercenaries in the world.

This group's official designation with the United States government is the Association of Privatized American Pistoleers.

Among their members and governing body they are colloquially known as...

The Gunfighters Guild.

AMONG COLLEAGUES AND RIVALS

CHAPTER ONE

CHRIST CHURCH
28 BULL STREET,
JOHNSON SQUARE
SAVANNAH, GEORGIA
MARCH 1, 1866

Dear Claramay,

676 days ago, we engaged ourselves in a covenant beyond the comprehension of men. And one day prior, 677 days before this day, I set the seal of you upon my heart. It strikes me, love: that in the space of a single day nestled among the willow wood near the pond where I spent all my childish years, your palm fell into mine, and we turned to each other, facing our backs to rules and the fractured society that demands them. You kissed me, and we became women together. You set your hands on my face, and twenty-two hours later we banded our hearts and damned the world.

We damn it still.

You damned it in your own reserved way.

And I am sending you this letter because I must damn it in mine.

For my life, I will love you. Dreaming you to life while I sleep, waking to remember that it was for a greater purpose that I chose this path for myself. In a way, I am choosing it for you too, love. I have no misgivings that your tears will run the dark shade of this ink pale and that while you cry, you shall look as beautiful and innocent as you ever have in sorrow or in rain.

And I know and I know.

I know you will disbelieve the words you are reading. You will question the validity of the letter. You will think that perhaps my father found a way to block this grand romance we have for 677 days grown in the secret garden of the heart we share. The love we so patiently and quietly grew. You will think to yourself, "How can she do this?"

It will hurt you to know that I do it with ease. But I say it all the same, Clara, because for 677 days only a single lie passed from me to you. I will not speak a second. I will not break that promise. A small consolation, I know, with you now holding the note that will break the single greatest promise I have ever made. We waited together for today. Planned. Schemed with smiles on our faces to wed one another among lilies and lupins and sunflowers, encircled by the little barricade of roses whose thorns first showed me the color of your blood. And with this papercut, I know and I know, I will pierce the heart of the woman I wanted to share the whole of my life with. The woman I still wish to spend the rest of my life with. But I am called away unto greater purpose than a marital pact, by a voice that bids me come and take a close walk with a master stranger than Death.

Even without knowing the exact time your eye falls upon the page, hours after I have written it, I feel your heartbreak. I feel it now, and I feel it in the moment which you are now living. I will feel it forever. And that is mine to endure —the shattering of you—for all the measure of time and all the measure of me.

For hours and hours, you will hate me. Curse me. Damn me as you have damned the rest.

And in days and weeks and perhaps the length of years, there will come a time when you bid me hurry back.

A lesser woman would sink into that feeling, find herself drawn like an anchor into the deep sea of you and dragged against the current of what must be, if only to touch the love of you again.

I am not a lesser woman.

It is a credit to you, a marker of the worth residing within you, Clara, that I take the time to pen my intent before I make my mark on the world. No. That is the voice of humility driven into me by my father's deliberate mellowing of the ferocity living within me.

I will not make a mark, Claramay.

I will change the world. All of it, for all time.

I see so clearly the way and have now the patron who has given me the vision by which it can be accomplished. And unlike all other men, who have for so long asked me to speak softly and curtsy and allow them in greeting to kiss the gloved hand that has for 677 days belonged to you, this man—this High Priest—bids me to do none of these things. For where all other men demand my submission, this man requires my ascension.

And so, I will refuse the great depths of your love where I would have happily drowned for all the remainder of my years. I leave our shore, pass by our secret garden, to rise. To fly and fly and then plunge with talons unfurled to wound the skin of the world where we have shared our happiest seasons.

You have been the grateful spring of my life, twice over carrying me through hot summers and through the many-colored fields of autumn, and now the winter of us has come quickly, oh so quickly, Claramay. And more than just the winter of our romance and love, but a winter to cover all things, all loves, and all lives. A bright, cold reckoning that I want you to see and know and have. I need you to see. It is so important that you know and take this great gift that I go now to make for you at the expense of all that we might have shared. I trade now our dreamed future for a future that can be greater than any dream.

It comes at not only the expense of our joy but at

the cost of all of me—meaning us. Now and forever and always and Claramay, and every other word that means eternity. You and you and you, only you; it is all for you that I shatter my heart, and in doing so, shatter the heart we share.

Let your anger blossom, spring. Let it flourish in our secret garden. Hate me for a time, for at the root of it I know is planted a passion which the sunbeam cannot wither, nor can many waters drown it. A love that can subsist beyond the winter of our loss and the winter of all I will gain in the hour of my accomplishment.

Claramay, do not mourn me a loss. Think I am gone, remember my name, and wait for me.

For as long as my life was my own, I gave it to you. I, Gwendolyn Pierce Butler, love you, Claramay Rose Diamine. I leave the name and the woman it named behind, but always taking with me the dream of you.

With all my love and no regret,
Gwenny

CHAPTER TWO

NEW ORLEANS, LOUISIANA
MARCH 9, 1866

S ven Erickson and Larry Cornish rode into New Orleans a pair of men living in the uncertainty of what would come next, robed in the certain protection of each other. Four months had passed since what would prove to be their first martial engagement, when they had challenged one another to a contest of the gun, only to find that neither could fire. For they had looked into each other's eyes and found within the other person the segment of themselves they had for years not known they had been missing. And so, assaulted by love at first sight, the gunfighters yielded to one another. Surrendering to passion in an East Texas thicket, they wove their hearts and bodies together—all while knowing it could cost them their lives.

"I won't be without it," Sven had said, lying near the fire they had built together, scratching his ribs and shaking his head. He was a big man. Tall and handsome, thick as a bull all over and smiling always, unless the demon of the bottle had its hold on him.

"The Guild rules," said Larry Cornish. Average in every way to the world—height, eyes, build and color of hair—and in every measure of the things the world could not appreciate, Sven found this man exceptional.

"I am the fastest gun alive, Larry, my love," he said, so cool and so charming. Gentle and refined. "There is nothing I cannot keep that I *decide* to keep. The Guild has rules a hundred years old. You, I have had for less than a year. And if the Guild tries to draw us apart, there is no contest as to which side I shall choose and which I shall burn."

And there, three months prior to their riding into New Orleans to answer for their love and their disregard for the Guild's laws, Sven Erickson and Larry Cornish lay together in the cold December night, drawing from each other pleasure and passion bright and hot as sun fire. Each kiss an ember. Every word a spark. They must have known each other before meeting, and the love they made proved it over and over. Their bodies had moved together with years and years and perhaps decades of life together they had not yet lived. Wholly satisfied by each embrace, they both found themselves wanting more.

Along the sodden road that ran hard and straight toward New Orleans, riding by his love's side, Sven said, "You are everything to me, Larry Cornish."

Larry did not look, answering, "And you to me."

The only thing more plain than their affection for each other was the road before them. Sven rode Midnight, a thoroughbred Missouri Fox Trotter, so named for the way his coat caught the moon. Larry rode Heartbeat, a Saddlebred given to him by a widower after his wife, the horse's previous rider, had died. The man could no longer bear the reminder of all he had lost.

Larry had protested the widower's gift. "I will pay an honest price."

The widower, so despondent, threw in the tack and saddle too, saying, "Take it all. The full cost is the promise you will make."

"Promise?"

"Treat him well and take him far away. And never come back."

New Orleans lay cloaked in a gloomy fog rolling from the black waters of the Mississippi River, hooded in the pall of wood smoke rising from steamboat stacks and tripod fires. Shot all through the hazy gloam were the city's gas lamps, burning like a constellation belt never to rise higher than the horizon. Streets of moonstruck mud snaked that way and this, where they came to bunch, coiling to a grander path cut from cobblestone. The light of the lamps wavered upon the stone, giving them the quality of brass and bronze and sterling silver. The road was illuminated in such a way that it might lead to the throne of Heaven or Valhalla or whatever eternity awaits every wandering soul dreaming of what the end might be. The path all walk: those who rush without fear and those who steadily step, hoping Death's patience will last a year or a day, perhaps only an hour.

Midnight and Heartbeat stuttered when their iron-shod hooves came to clap upon the shining stone. The riders, understanding the trepidation, offered their horses encouraging words and then gave each other wary looks.

"What do you think they will say?" asked Sven, letting Midnight take all the slack from the reins, letting the horse have his way.

"Rebuke, love," said Larry. "Our choice halts progression. Halts the game."

"There you go worrying," said Sven.

"Worry keeps us alive."

"We keep each other alive. And if any of these silver-pinned fucks try to claim your life or mine," Sven laughed, pure menace in the sound.

"I care so little for the whole of the world, now that you have become the world to me. So, do not fret, husband. If the House of the Gun proves to be a place of contest, I assure you, ours will be the night."

"Contest is certain," said Larry, setting himself straight once again in the saddle. He unbuttoned his sleeves, rolling each up slowly, so that the dark lime and gold window-paned twill folded in on itself to reveal slender arms corded with quick muscle. "The outcome, less so." Heartbeat chuffed, his mane shaking away the heat and sweat accosting him. Skin rippling against a fresh onset of flies, he shook again, displeased.

"You know what," said Sven, guiding Midnight closer to his husband. He placed a hand on Larry's arm, curling his hand around the wrist. "Of all the things I love about you, it is your pessimism I love the least."

"You will keep loving it all the same," said Larry, giving a rare grin.

"Yes, sir," said Sven, giving him a squeeze. "I am happy to obey. In any case, the Gold Pins will hear our reasoning. Judge us fair, I think."

"We could still yield."

Sven squeezed again, harder this time. "No," he said. "I do not yield. Not while I have you. Not until the end."

The two men fell silent a moment, looking into the other's eyes.

"You did not fall in love with caution or safety. You fell in love with me," said Sven, fierce and brash and bold.

"Yes," said Larry. "Yes." Again, with zeal.

Further down the length of the cobblestone road, tracing the dark, southwesterly bulge of massive Lake Pontchartrain, the gaslighted streets began to rumble and peal with the sound of drums and fiddles and fifes and horns. The road narrowed, forking like a shimmering stone river spraying to delta. Soiled doves called down from cathouses painted green and gold and the kind of blue found in the farthest reach of a summer day sky. Some made promises of love and unforgettable nights, others brandished their breasts or pressed their naked torsos against covered balconies so that the tuft of their pubis could be spied. Larry and Sven rode, smiling and tipping their hats and shaking their heads. Well-to-do Creole men in various stages of lechery and dressed in fine linen suits called up to the women, throwing them kisses and making promises of their own.

A foppish youth, no older than twenty-five by the look of him, drunkenly challenged a Black man leaving one of the buildings to a knife fight for some unknown offense. Sven and Larry rode between challenger and challenged, which gave the youth's friends enough time to think better of what might happen should the contest be had. And, pulling the young man away, the friends soothed his temper with a bottle of wine. The young man drank and suddenly laughed, the wine spraying from his lips, soiling his silk shirt with a wash of red.

One friend lifted his voice: "Better the color on you than out of you, Maurice!" They carried on with their jesting down a length of dark alleyway, unafraid of the night or the fog or the life ahead of them.

Sven watched them. Wondered where they were going and how long their fraternity might last.

Larry, who saw Sven looking, said, "Lucky."

He turned and winked at Larry. "Not nearly as lucky as us."

They rode together, admiring the narrow streets, the music filling them, and the people living with passions thrown high. The city of New Orleans, from the bend of the Mississippi to the banks of Pontchartrain, boiled with life and fervor and the unrelenting will to cast all care into the void of the night—a city that would live forever. The gunslingers took it all in, pointing out the midnight shops selling their wares and the roiling saloons that populated the churning maelstrom that was French Quarter. Bourbon Street, the most furious section of the happy storm, was festooned with flags of purple and gold and trimmed in tassels of green. The flags hung from balconies and flagpoles and the shoulders of a naked man who walked among the world with the colors of the city like a cape. In the windows of restaurants were men and women having fine meals long past midnight. And in the faces of every living person was the sheer, drunken bliss served only in the rarest of places, none rarer than this.

Eventually the city's cobblestones ebbed away, and they followed the chopped-up, muddy road leading to a large plantation lot where stood the white colonnades along the edifice of the House of the Gun. A long, wrought iron fence, skirted with manicured hedges and trimmed in thin leaf ivy, ran straight across the property, where it's torchlit gate stood open, attended by a single man holding a rifle.

"Good evening, gentleman," said the attendant as the riders dismounted. He was short, lean, and bespectacled by gold-rimmed glasses that flashed bright as harvest moons when they caught the torchlight. Tipping his hat, he did not wait for Larry and Sven to respond. "This is the House of the Gun. Only those invited or numbered by silver pin may go beyond."

Sven flipped over the lapel of his coat to reveal the sterling metal, etched simply with the number eleven. "My name is Sven Erickson. I am the Eleven."

The attendant nodded. "Ah," he said, understanding. "Mr. Erickson, which must make you—?"

"Larry Cornish," said Larry, unmoving. "The Nine."

"Certainly, Mr. Cornish." The attendant looked over his shoulder. "My stableboy will be back soon to collect your horses." He looked back to the two gunslingers. He was grinning. "Many have arrived tonight and are awaiting you. And, if I may be so bold, sirs, the story of your love has spread all throughout the guildfolk. And, please, if I may be even bolder without breaking my vow of impartiality, might I say: I am rooting for you."

"Will they at least hear us out?" asked Sven, suddenly cold and serious.

"I couldn't hardly guess, Mr. Erickson," said the attendant. "But if you pressed me on it, I would guess the Gold Pins would hear you fair."

"He hopes they will," said Larry, tilting his head to indicate Sven to the attendant.

"I know the rules, gateman," said Sven. "You are not permitted to tell us your name. Nor where you come from or anything about yourself. You can say nothing about any person who has come through this gate that might provide an advantage to any potential contender to their pin. And you are not allowed to leave this post unless directly commanded by your superiors inside."

"That's the long of it."

"And here's the short of it," said Sven, his voice chipped with ice. "You hear the sound of battle coming from the House of the Gun tonight, abandon your post."

"Sir?"

"Hear me, son," Sven approached and set Midnight's reins into the gateman's hand. "If circumstance requires me to shoot my way out of this place, I will do it. And if you, in your duty, set yourself between me and my husband's flight, I will kill you. I would lose sleep over it, certainly... but make no mistake, you'll be dead before you hit the ground."

The gateman took the reins and, looking into the face of Sven Erickson, made no indication of what choice he would make.

Sven put one of his big hands on the young man's shoulder as he passed him by, through the gate. "Don't make me do it, kid."

Larry handed his reins over too. "Hear him," he said to the gateman. "Live."

The gunslingers, side by side, sauntered up the straight-as-a-truth-teller pathway made of pebble stones toward the white, many-windowed plantation house. Sven took Larry by the hand, lacing their fingers together. And as they passed beneath a fairy-tale-like arch crafted by two oak trees reaching high above and into one another, he squeezed his lover's hand tightly. Larry squeezed back. Then, their fingers relaxed, their hands slipping loose as they approached a pair of great, green doors banded in iron: the entry to the House of the Gun.

"I love you, Larry Cornish," said Sven, reaching to knock.

"And I you," said Larry. "And I you."

CHAPTER THREE

THE HOUSE OF THE GUN
NEW ORLEANS, LOUISIANA
MARCH 9, 1866

The door opened before Sven's fist had a chance to fall, slow and heavy and soundless. Standing in the width of the gap, wearing a funeral black tuxedo and looming like a vulture, was amber-eyed Boris Kane. His head shined smooth and bright as a boiled egg, and that was all that shined about him. He rarely smiled, was always polite, as if all his mirth had been replaced with a fierce love of formality. "Mr. Erickson," he said. Then, he slanted those bright eyes over to Larry. "And Mr. Cornish. You are expected."

Larry nodded.

"Boris," said Sven, then went to step over the door's threshold.

Boris put up a hand, palm facing the two

gunfighters. "I do beg your pardon, Mr. Erickson, but I have been instructed by the Gold Pins to request your guns *before* you enter. And though I am a servant of tradition, I am still a higher servant of those who ensure those traditions are upheld. So, if you please…" The man twisted his upturned palm, waiting to accept.

"Why?" asked Larry.

Boris nodded, as if he had expected the question. "Mine is not to ask how and why, but to do and die, Mr. Cornish. Now, if you would, please."

"You know, Boris, this is my third time at one of these convocations," said Sven, his voice relaxed. Charming. "I never have asked, what happens if we refuse to surrender our guns to you?"

Boris smiled, and somehow it made him seem older. Possessed by fatigue. "I would allow you entry, of course, unmolested."

"Oh, well then…"

"You would, of course, be shot on sight by one of the Gold Pins the moment you entered the drawing room, where the rest of the unarmed guildfolk await. One," said Boris, who then looked up in consideration, then back into Sven's eyes. "Perhaps all three."

Larry unholstered his gun and, handing it to Boris, gave Sven a frustrated look. "Could have told you that."

Sven gave up his gun too, smiling big at

Larry. "Yeah, but you love me. You might lie to me to make me feel better."

"Never," said Larry, so serious it stole all the fun from Sven's joke.

"Gentleman," Boris interrupted, clutching their pistols in his hands, "I invite you inside, into the House of the Gun, and proclaim you welcome to this convocation, where you shall walk under Guild protection and hospitality."

And walk they did, into the House of the Gun, shoulder to shoulder and with hearts knotted across the space between them—uncertain, unarmed, and unafraid. The palatial home opened into a grand space with a marble floor of black and white squares. Every stone was slick and shining, as though it had just been drawn out of a clear, shallow stream. A winding stairwell rose to their right, running to the second-story landing like the biggest goddamn fancy corkscrew a person would ever see. To their left, on a long wall wainscoted in fine panels from chair rail to marble floor, hung oil paintings of each and every gunslinger who had worn a gold pin, all the way back to General Alexander Castlemaine, who had founded this branch of the Guild during the Revolutionary War. The portraits of the former champions, all the first among gunfighter equals, had been numbered in threes. Their faces were of varying colors running the whole spectrum of human flesh.

There were men and women, Native people, and immigrants, all of them equal here. For when it came to the House of the Gun, the only prejudice accepted was that of weapon caliber, make, and model. Below the portraits, framed in ebony wood, were brass plates that bore the champion's name and the year they traded in a silver pin for one of a rarer color.

Sven always looked at the paintings as he walked slowly toward the drawing room, examining the gunfighters dressed in velvety reds and purples, summer grass greens, and blues as deep as the ocean the Swede had crossed to reach this new world. This place where Sven had chased the immigrant's opportunity. Where Larry Cornish had changed his life. His new homeland: America.

"Mint," said Larry, breaking the silence between the syncopated sound of their steps.

"Yeah," said Sven, knowing it was Larry's favorite. "Smells nice."

The happy sound of comradery and jests fluttered toward them from beyond the wall. The gunfighters turned left into the drawing room and paused in the doorway. Greater than two dozen souls stood within, some of them smoking, others drinking from fine silver cups perched at their lips, some sitting or leaning upon the sofas or standing upon the white sable rugs that carpeted the marble floor—the collective whole of the ranks of the Gunfighters Guild. Every eye slashed to meet them. All of them, Silver and Gold Pins alike, stared at the two men who had entered. Laughter ebbed slowly. The conversations slowed too, until there was only the sound of silence and the silent hammering of hearts ready to bleed for nothing more than the contest of their association.

And it was in this way that Larry was no longer like his gunfighter ilk. No more did the game hold his highest priority. There was a time he had chased the pin of the One with the unquenchable fire that is happily unknown to those born without the competitor's defect. But in place of a pin upon his chest, Larry had inscribed a name on his heart.

Sven, his love for Larry second to no living force in the world, still desperately desired to be revered among the rest of the Guild, to be the fastest hand that had ever drawn a gun. Not only in his time, but all time. To be more than a gunfighter. More than a man. A legend. This was Sven's way, Larry knew that. It had been the initial spark of their mutual attraction. And because Larry Cornish loved the whole of Sven Erickson, he would never ask the man to be any way but that which he was.

"The Nine," announced Boris from behind them. "And the Eleven."

From out of the drawing room came a dark-haired figure, gliding gracefully through the portrait-still crowd. Wrapped in emerald silk with a sash of fire-red fox fur across one shoulder and a golden pin upon her breast, she wore her ferocity as a queen wears a crown.

"There you are," she said, her voice bright as the green-blue storm of her eyes.

"Belle," said Sven.

"Sven Erickson," said Belle Starr, one-third of the Gold Pin rank. She approached and leaned out her chin.

Sven kissed her lightly on the cheek.

She smiled. "And Larry Cornish."

Larry nodded. "Ms. Starr."

Lowering her voice playfully, she said, "You know, of all the problems and contests I have been required to settle at this convocation, this one has the potential to make me the happiest. Now," she said and paused, as if only now noticing the heavy silence wreathing the room. She turned to the onlookers, all leaning their ears to try and hear the conversation. "Please, friends," she said, lifting her voice. "Guild business will begin shortly. For now, return to your wine and whiskey and fellowship."

As slowly as it had ebbed, a fresh wash of talk spilled over in the drawing room.

"Belle—"

"No, Sven. Me first, or have you forgotten the way of things?" She shoved the big Swede in the chest and tilted her head slightly. "You didn't come here to yield, did you."

"No," said Larry.

Belle's smile expanded, somehow stealing a little of the happiness in her. "I thought not. Which means you are hindering the game."

"I am the Eleven," began Sven. "Still able to be challenged. Willing."

"I see," said Belle. "And what say you, Nine? You will not yield. That is your right. No one can take that from you. But will you attempt to advance?"

Larry looked over her shoulder, into a room of killers. So certain about Sven and so uncertain about himself. "No rule about advancing."

"No written rule," said Belle.

"Only written rules matter."

Her eyes widened, a little shocked and a little offended. "Oh, and will you tell me the nature of the game, Larry? You understand that it is not beyond me to write a new rule...right now...in this very place."

"Rule of three," said Larry, his words coming quick.

"Larry," said Sven, frustrated.

"That's right," said Belle, ignoring Sven. "Three Gold Pins to make one new rule or cast a judgment. You have always been a smart man, Larry Cornish. A bookworm through one side of the apple and out the other. Eight through One are happy for you both to stand pat, but look at those behind me. Those whose pins number from the Twelve to the Twenty-five. Look at the hunger in their eyes, and those eyes looking at you," she said, watching Larry and Sven scan the room. "Yes," she continued, "These, your eager opponents. Each of them ready and willing to strike at two men who believe their affection for one another supersedes the game and those who play it. Now, I understand your position. Sven, you want to continue to play. And you, unyielding Larry, no longer wish to advance, but you cannot use up your single yield for the Ten, because that means you will have no yield to offer Sven. What to do then, Larry. *What to do?*" Belle reached up and patted both men on the shoulder at the same time. "But let us put away all the numbers for now, all save one. The number that constitutes all my problems tonight: two. The two of you with your game-locking love. The two Gold Pins who already want to write a rule to force you to advance. The two patrons here, both wishing to buy our services. And, my word, the Two has made a challenge on the One."

"Chelsea Vermillion," said Sven, perhaps too softly. "He's here?"

Belle nodded and stroked the fur set across her bosom. "Gifted me this as a way of apologizing for being unfindable for near a decade. I accepted the fur and have yet to accept the apology.”

“Oliver Maine?” asked Larry.

“Here, in the flesh,” said Belle, rolling her eyes up as if in ecstasy. “And, boys, let me tell you, I saw him draw down on Calico Pip for the Two. There he is, wearing it now.” She opened her shoulder and gestured to a brown-haired man who was making his way through the French doors leading outside. His skin, tanned like fine leather, set off the green-gold fire of his eyes. And even among the dangerous crowd of the world’s most dangerous pistoleers, dressed all in black save for the shining silver polish of his revolver, Maine moved with the high-shouldered confidence afforded to the greatest among equals. Looking him over, she let out a long sigh. “Even missing one hand, he is every inch the threat he claims to be.”

Sven leaned close to Belle, intrigued. “So, why did Vermillion—”

“He prefers to be called ‘Red,’ Mr. Erickson. And because he is the One, I will ask you grant him that courtesy even outside his company.”

Sven rolled his eyes. “Fine. Did Red say why he’s all of a sudden back for this challenge? He ducked Calico Pip for years.”

Belle laughed. “Ducked? Red doesn’t duck anyone, big boy. Red was doing him a favor, letting time either mature the art of Pip’s draw or allow Red to grow slower in his old age. It wasn't fear, it was charity. As the One, that is his prerogative."

"When?" asked Larry.

"Maine asked for midnight," said Belle, dreamy and aloof. "Under the light of the moon. Like the contests of old." She turned back to Larry, her eyes suddenly filled with patience, and something like understanding. "Your heart no longer belongs to the game. It belongs to your Sven. And that is a beautiful thing…. Perhaps then, your only recourse is to retire."

"No," said Sven.

Belle sniffed a surprised laugh. "You may make choices for Larry in life, Sven, but when it comes to the game, the choice is his. And his alone."

Larry looked to Sven.

He silently shook his head at Larry.

"Retire and lose all the pin's protection," said Larry.

"Correct," replied Belle. "Any Pin looking to increase their reputation will come after you and will not be required to approach you within the rules. Several could even gang up on you, and I assume they would, knowing how dangerous you are."

"Their lives would be forfeit," said Sven, eyes widening and face reddening.

"Only if Larry becomes your patron," said

Belle. "I know he's the brains, Sven, but you know better than this. And, within the *written rules*, a retired member must pay a guild-set price for a current member. If it were any other way, money would corrupt the game we all, except Larry here, love so well."

"Listen, Belle—"

"Sven, honey, I've said all there is to say on the matter and given you all the information I can without giving advantage. Larry knows his options. You know your way. It's time for guild business soon, so I suggest you take the time to talk it through."

"Thank you, Ms. Starr," said Larry, solemn and resigned.

Belle placed a hand on his cheek, a touch so soft never a living person would have believed the woman had killed her way to the top of the Guild rank before the age of thirty. "Best of luck, love," she said, then looked to Sven. "And you too, gunfighter."

Sven and Larry watched her saunter back into the crowd as each and every pistoleer moved from her path like the earth opening before the emerald stream of her dress.

"Hadn't considered retirement," said Larry.

"And we're not considering it now," said Sven.

"We are."

Sven ran his tongue over his teeth, frustrated.

"Say you retire, and for the sake of the argument, let's say no one ever comes after you, which is the longest fucking longshot in the history of anything; if I am hired on with a patron, I will be forced to go where they send me. If I am sent away from you...who will be there to help you, should you need it?" He looked his husband in the eyes, throwing all the weight of his concern and fear of loss into his voice. "If I am gone, who will take care of you?"

"I am capable."

"Yes," said Sven. "And mine."

"Yours," said Larry.

"Challenge the Eight," said Sven, his words desperate. "I will challenge Ten. That will buy us time to figure this out. That will allow me to protect you from behind. We just need more time."

"Paul Moody is Eight. Seen him draw." Larry turned away. "He is my better."

"Fuck that," Sven's anger came up, boiling. "You can't think that way."

"I do, husband," said Larry. "Moody is faster. Burns like you to be the best. Facing him means death."

"Then I'll kill the Ten, and you can yield to me—"

"Would then be forced to face every upcoming gun. No. Retirement: the only option."

Sven took a step, bringing himself to stand

before his husband. "If we could just buy more—"

From over the cavalcade of conversations and bawdy laughter and drinking and threats and jests came the voice of Belle Starr. She spun around gracefully, lifting a single hand in the air so that all attention came to focus on emerald silk and fox fur and the woman wrapped within them. "The time for iron and steel and nickel and brass is set aside," she began. The words were an invocation older than the country of which she was a citizen. Older than guns or the gunpowder they used. "Silver and gold, brothers and sisters. Silver and gold, peace and fellowship."

"No more time, love," said Larry, placing a hand on Sven's shoulder. And he gazed at his husband with blue eyes, the color of merciless waters, unapologetic in their sorrow.

Belle's voice rose again, hot and excited, with all the power of a Valkyrie's war cry. "Gold and silver, the colors of our association and the only color of currency we have ever accepted!"

The crowd gave a laugh, many of the gunfighters nodding.

"Silver Pins, I am of the Gold, and I welcome you here to this, your house, that we might bear together the business of our convocation. We will settle disputes, lay naked the law, and," she slashed her eyes left and right for the sake of mock intrigue, "for the first time in over twenty years, a challenge for the pin of the One has been issued...*and tonight will see it settled*!"

There was a leap of sound from the crowd, all of the gunfighters shouting in one voice.

"And among us tonight, two patrons—one coming by way of Texas and the other who calls grand New Orleans her home—seek to buy the service that we alone can provide. Silver and Gold, let me introduce to you first to New Orleans madam of Le Champ de Fleurs de Pavot, Reine Silvia Louis.

The crowd cheered and whooped as a blonde woman dressed in a flowing French dress of crimson silks and satins, black cotton and lace with shining flowers of black jet emblazoned upon her bosom, waved a gloved hand.

"Queen of the many flowered field, we welcome you and will hear your petition after our contest," said Belle, who then turned to look across the room. "And second to gain our audience is a man of whom I am certain you have all heard. Judge Hezekiah Ellison of the infamous and enigmatic Peregrine Estate, you have our sincere welcome!"

Thick as he was, the brown suit he wore made the bald Judge look more like a barrel than a man. He was not quite as tall as Sven but certainly matching him in bulk. A smoking pipe, big and curved with a bowl shaped like an acorn, hung from his lips and over his black beard. He gave a curt nod.

"And," said Belle, lengthening the word like a carnival crier. "I know there has come a complaint, from the high and low of the Gold and Silver, regarding the relationship that has developed between Larry Cornish, the Nine, and his lover Sven Erickson, the Eleven."

At those words, there came no shout, cry, or bellow but only a long silence. And again, the group eye of the room came to fall upon the gunslingers Nine and Eleven.

"Some of you cry collusion, and others, more ignorant and barbaric in your thinking, grasp at bigotry, proclaiming that it is you who should be able to determine the shape of love in the world." Belle's eyes grew cold, frosting her levity, and her voice chipped with ice. "But hear me when I say, Silver and Gold, and Gold and Silver, that in the House of the Gun, these *bigotries* die at the threshold step. Your position on their affection goes unacknowledged. It is irrelevant here. And any man or woman who believes they know better or wishes it to be different may now, with the wager of their silver pin and life, test this Gold Pin. I lay myself open to challenge."

There was a long moment of absolute silence as her eyes sought out anyone who dared answer her challenge. But she proved too dangerous a propositioner for the room of otherwise unflappable gunslingers.

"Speak for contest now," said Belle, with a look that killed the thrill-seek within every gunfighting daredevil in the room. "For I will not offer a second time."

After the span of a few more moments, empty of all protest and challenge, Belle's sweet, charming smile returned. "Guess you aren't half as dumb as you look," she said.

The silence vanished in the sunlight-bright laughter of every unarmed Silver Pin in the room.

"Now," Belle hollered over the sound of all tension relieved, "let us be about our goddamn business!"

CHAPTER FOUR

The House of the Gun
New Orleans, Louisiana
March 9, 1866

The floor was opened first to Reine Silvia Louis. She spoke in English with a French accent, her words finer and more elegant than the red dress she wore. She was known all through New Orleans and further as the Queen of the Many Flowered Field. More than a madam, and with power greater than a senator, she had built from nothing an empire of brothels composed of incorporated men and women serving as paramours.

Sven and Larry sat at the back of the room, watching the greatest living madam in the United States, perhaps the world, address the greatest collective of gunfighters with the surety of a monarch and the deference of a diplomat.

"A trio of men, their coward faces hidden

behind bandana masks, assaulted a paramour," she said, twisting a red silk scarf in her hands. "Before this disgusting attack on his person, Claude St. Guy was a prize jewel upon the crown I have bled to build. They mutilated him. Slashed his face. Castrated him like an animal. His charm, which made him so famous to his many lovers, is broken now. The men I pay to protect my brothel fields were shot, their wives made widows, and their children half-orphaned." Queenly in every aspect, she lifted her chin to the crowd of thirty-five and said, with hatred, "I want the perpetrators of this act found and brought to me. And to ensure it is done well, I require the very best the House of the Gun has to offer. There is no need to discuss the price; I will pay it."

There was an inexhaustible fire within the woman, that much was clear.

"We should help her," said Sven, leaning slightly so that his shoulder touched Larry's.

"Problems of our own," Larry replied.

"You're right." Sven smirked. "We may not yet live to help another person ever again."

Larry slanted an eye to his husband. "Perhaps." He swallowed hard. "Perhaps not."

Sven knew that swallow. Knew the look in Larry's eye. "You have an idea."

Larry said nothing but looked back to the front of the room where a fire burned in the hearth and before its flames stood a woman on fire for justice.

"Thank you, Reine Silvia," said Belle. She sat just to the right of the hearth between two men. To the left was old Mute Caine, a small, slender man bearing thick scars all along the midnight black of his face. Despite the war-torn features of his flesh, the man carried in his eyes a calm, unhurried aspect. Neither Sven nor Larry knew much about Mute Caine aside from the telling of his rise to primacy thirty years back, having been the only previous champion to ever win the One pin by way of the top five pins all yielding without contest. And only two months after, he was elected by the Gold Pins to take the then vacant spot. The Bloodless Ascension someone had named his rise, but most folks knew the story more than they knew the moniker. However, they all knew the quiet man.

Opposite him, sitting with one leg crossed over the other and as relaxed as a snake can get, was Joshua Millsap. The man was the oldest among the Gold Pins, having won his seat in the 1820s amid the Guild's flintlock years. Millsap had been there, they said, watching the hand of President Andrew Jackson signing a document at the behest of his friend Aaron Burr which legitimized the Gunfighters Guild as a lawful association of duelists within the United States.

"Our hearts go out to you," said Millsap to

the madam. "Certainly our guns will go, too. However, first we will hear Judge Ellison's request, that each Pin will have a chance to choose your plight, the Judge's, or no plight at all."

Reine Silvia Louis gave a delicate nod, then made her way to a wingback chair not too far from the hearth, the silks of her skirt swishing amid the quiet gunslingers and the crackling of the fire.

"Judge Ellison, if you please," said Belle, inviting him to gather the audience of the room.

And over he strode, his footfalls heavy, his gray eyes shimmering in the wavering hearth-sent light. Before he reached the front of the room, as he walked among the gunslingers, he began to speak with a voice like thunder and a passion greater than the storm.

"My name is Hezekiah Ellison. And I am the falconer of the Peregrine Estate. I am a man of means, though not so great as to afford more than one of you for this particular mission, which I will openly attest offers little to no fame, for much of the work my people do is done in secret. That is the way of it. There is no great earthly reward should we find success. Only money. That which spends too quickly and refuses to go with you, wherever you go, should you die. And a promise: that if you come to work with me, you will see things that will change your understanding of the world; and in that world, you will have made a difference." He reached the hearth, turned, and crossed his big arms over his chest, standing like some bearded colossus darkened by the fire of the sun.

"There was a time when I would never have considered coming to this place, for I believe that the whole span of those who have ever been pinned, only to be killed, or killed another to gain a higher pin, have wasted the blood of their lives on vain conquest. I speak plainly. Lie only when life requires it. And here, before this death-bringing collective of duelists, I admit that while I have never loved your contest, I can certainly appreciate your need for it. I understand the competition living inside each and every one of you; the ache for challenge, the harrowed longing to know the height of the gambler's dice-roll and the performer's curtain call. What it means for you to walk upon the blade-thin bridge that leads from nothing to everything. In short, Silver Pins, though I hate your game, I understand the reason you play it."

Ellison took a breath, chewed his cheek in quiet contemplation, as if he were mulling in his own study and not within the House of the Gun. "I cannot tell you my business, lest you sign on with me. I am that kind of employer. My needs are like the Grand Canyon; they're hole-in-the-ground simple but overwhelmingly deep. I require an agent of the greatest capability, and I do not give a damn which number they brandish upon their chest." With a graceful gesture, he drew the eyes of the gunfighters over to Reine Silvia Louis. "Madam Louis's money will stretch further to wealth than what I can afford, and she only requires you to find the men who deserve to die for what they did to Mr. St. Guy. There will be honor and greater fortune in her assignment than mine." He leaned forward, tipping at the waist. "But not greater danger. Do not accept my bid if the sum of your desire is to make money and live as you have always lived. I tell you truly, if you come with me, you will be changed by the things witnessed and by the actions my company requires."

And with that, the fire inside the man's eyes diminished. He popped his pipe back into his mouth and began to smoke again.

"Judge Ellison," said Joshua Millsap, cool and easy, "while we respect any patron's desire to maintain a certain level of discretion, I am afraid that your statement's foggy nature provides too great an obfuscation for any Silver Pin to accept or Gold Pin to compel."

"My business," said Ellison, his tone sharp and serious, "is my business. And I know for a fact, for a goddamn hellfire and damnation fact, that my enemies hire out to you such as I am doing now. I would not have them know my plans or let it reach them that I was here, seeking help. But I am running out of options. And manpower."

Belle Starr leaned forward in her chair, her voice the pure definition of boldness and grace. "This is the House of the Gun, Hezekiah. It is our sacred place. Here we follow a codified set of rules. One of which is this: That which is heard in the House of the Gun is for the House of the Gun. Your secrets, your hatreds, your vulnerabilities, you may voice all of them there. Joshua has the right of it. Your request for a gunhand is too vague."

As Ellison and Starr went back and forth on the definition of vague, Larry leaned over to Sven. "This is how we buy time. You with the Judge. Me with the madam."

"Apart?" said Sven, the word bitter in his mouth.

"You wanted time. Show the Guild I am still active. I will take this job. You the other. St. Guy deserves vengeance. Ellison needs the best.

"Lover, I don't want—"

Larry placed a firm hand atop Sven's. Though it was smaller, it squeezed with a vice-like strength. "Trust. Now."

Sven gazed long and hard into Larry's eyes, his jaw working like a piston. "You're sure?"

Larry made no indication of yes or no, only looking at him in silent command.

"You cannot expect," said Millsap, breaking in again to argue with Judge Ellison, "one of our gunhands to sign on for what might be an assassination attempt on a political figure, or a crime upon which would chafe their personal moral—"

"I will accept," said Sven, unfolding out of his chair to stand the tallest man in the room.

"The house recognizes the Eleven," said Belle Starr, holding to tradition. "Speak your terms, Silver Pin."

Sven nodded to Belle, then looked to Ellison. "My name is Sven Erickson, and among my colleagues am I ranked Eleven of Twenty-Five. I am the fastest draw in this room, which is to admit to being the fastest in the world. I am more accurate than any hand sitting or standing before you. The members of this association believe I am attempting to protect my husband—Larry Cornish, the Nine—from their challenges." Sven looked at Larry, sniffed a laugh. "They are wrong. I am not protecting Larry from them; I am protecting them from Larry."

Muffled chuckles and discontented grumbles went through the room.

Sven gave them no mind. "If you promise me, Judge Ellison, that you will not require me to harm a child or work to help the cause of any former or present Confederate, or keep me from the whiskey I love, then on behalf of all within the House of the Gun, I say, thank you."

A little smirk slashed white in Ellison's black beard. "Thank you? For what?"

Sven let the charm melt from his face as he stared into the eyes of every Silver Pin looking his way. "For taking me as your gunfighter. In doing so, you have saved the life of every motherfucker in this room who conspired against my husband."

A murmur shuddered through the room. The Fifteen Pin, Kate Rice-McMasters, shot out of her chair and pointed an accusing finger at Sven. "Fuck you, Erickson! Horner at the Twelve might be afraid to fight you, but I'm sure as shit not."

At this, Michael Horner, the Twelve Pin, who had been quietly stirring his sherry cobbler cocktail and listening, lifted a black eyebrow set above a green eye and pursed his lips. "I'm sorry, Katie, what was that? Did you say afraid? It's difficult to hear you from three pins away."

"Fuck you, too, Horner!"

"Aw, sit down, Kate, you hot-blooded pup," said Daniel 'Five-Drinks-Deep' Willis, the Fourteen, who was old enough to be her father and considered by many to be a champion in-waiting. The pale Carolina tobacco farmer turned gunfighter leaned his slender frame against the wall and knocked back a shot of the House whiskey.

Then came the braggart voices of every Pin from Twelve to Twenty-Five, all of them slinging cusses and accusations and challenges, buzzing louder than a hornet's nest. Larry and Sven kept quiet, so too did the likes of Paul Moody, the Eight, all the way up the line to the Three.

Among the thirteen riled-up gunfighters, fists were raised and blows were ready to be thrown, that was until Old Mute Cain, soundless as the inside of a buried coffin, stood up from his seat.

As he rose, every challenge and threat and boast died.

When silence and the crackling of the hearth-fire were all that were left, Mute Cain nodded to Hezekiah Ellison.

"Mr. Erickson," said the Judge, "I am certain you and husband come as a pair; however, I cannot afford you both."

"No," said Larry. "You cannot." Now it was Larry who stood up and, cold and steady as waters running beneath the sheet ice of a frozen river, appraised the room until his eyes fell upon the madam. "Larry Cornish, the Nine. Reine Silvia Louis, my service is yours."

"Thank you, Mr. Cornish," said the madam. "I require at least two more to suit my need."

Then, Paul Moody, whose only distinguishing feature was his acute plainness, stepped forward as he adjusted a silk puff tie of red and white that bisected the burgundy suit he was wearing.Then, he slid a palm to smooth his hair, slick and shining as olive oil. A whole production before he spoke. He wore a burgundy suit, set off in color by the barber pole bright stripes of red and white of his silk puff tie, with hair shining and slick as olive oil. "I am the Eight," he said, his voice delicate, almost feminine. "Paul Moody. I am, in fact, what in fiction what the rest of these pins claim to be."

Larry looked to Moody.

Moody looked right back, smiling. "Hello, Larry. It is good to see you again. Perhaps, after this little job, you will show me the courage you lacked in Kansas City."

"Paul Moody, I have heard of you," said Reine Silvia, nodding politely. "And? Who else will help me see the justice my people are owed?"

From the center of the room, there came a long, drawn-out slurping of a straw finding the bottom of a empty glass. "I am the Twelve," said Michael Horner, setting his empty cocktail glass on the table next to the leather couch he was on. With pale, grim eyes the color of limestone, he looked to Sven Erickson. "I will complete the trio you have requested, Reine Silvia. I have killed thirty-eight men, never once a woman or a child. Among that number are eleven bounty heads and thirteen former pin-bearers. If finding these men is your order, you'll find no greater hunting hound than the man you see before you."

"Is it settled then?" asked Belle, looking satisfied. Well pleased.

"I believe so," said Joshua Millsap. "Twelve, Nine, and Eight to conduct this New Orleans hunt. And the Eleven with the Judge."

"Excellent," said Belle. "And I hope this also settles the complaint regarding Mr. Erickson and Mr. Cornish. At least for now, yes?"

Old Mute Cain, as always, said nothing, only nodded.

Belle Starr clapped her hands together. "Marvelous. Now, let us all gather together outside, where twenty-six seats await us among the maple trees. That we might, for the first time in well on a decade, see the challenge for the One."

The Silver Maple Wood
House of the Gun
New Orleans, Louisiana
March 9, 1866

Oliver Maine leaned against the maple tree, smoking a cigarette and gazing upon the only red star in the night sky. It wasn't a star at all, he knew, but the planet Mars catching the light of the Sun from millions of miles away. He took his time with the cigarette. The leaf and paper, carefully rolled into a tight cylinder and filled with a tobacco he'd purchased the day before from a little tobacconist shop in the Vieux Carré, burned slow. The smoke was thick and serene. The flavor light, aromatic, tasting of mint. His mind was an empty space, a void as deep as the blackness surrounding shimmering Mars. Hands steady. Breathing unhurried. A trickle of sweat ran from his forehead, rolling toward his chin cool as a melting snowball.

The Silver Maple Wood was quiet. Shafts of moonlight shot through the canopy blue and bright, the cigarette smoke curling through the beams striping the leaning gunfighter. The face of the full moon smiled upon the man and the pin he wore, illuminating the silver icon etched with the number two.

Oliver Maine had lived a life before, having a wife and child taken by scarlet fever. This, his second life, was lived alone, certified in its worth by his desire to prove to the rest of the world that which he knew to be true. He had dedicated years and traveled for months on end, day after day risking all for the sake of finding this moment. To arrive here, in the Silver Maple Wood and see all his twenty-four prior risks pay off unto this, the now he had so passionately chased.

The chance to meet in contest—

"Evening, One-Hand," came the tenor voice of Chelsea Vermillion.

Oliver Maine kept his eyes on the sky, knowing. "Evening, One-Eye."

Vermillion approached, boots softly crunching amid the tree litter. "The rest of the convocation is inside, discussing matters outside of the business you and I have with each other. Makes me grateful." Vermillion leaned one shoulder onto the same tree Maine occupied. "I appreciate that we have some time together."

Maine sucked on the cigarette, now half done. And he breathed the smoke out through his words. "Oh? Why's that?"

"I was in Dallas, two months ago. Saw your contest with Pip."

Maine nodded. "He had an opportunity to yield. It did not make me happy to kill him."

Vermillion sniffed a laugh. "Nothing makes people like us happy, Oliver."

Maine turned, finally appraising Vermillion, seeing him up close for the first time. The gunfighter's skin was as cool as the moonlight, smooth shaven. One eye was blue as a summertime river, the other patched over in leather bleached white. He wore no hat, and his hair was thin, shining like silver spun thread. His suit was navy, the shirt and tie white as the eye patch. "You have the advantage now," said Maine, grinning. "You've seen me in action. Probably have a good guess at how fast I am, seen any tells I might have."

The old gunfighter glanced up, and with that river-blue eye evaluated Maine. "You've got no tells. And you're fast as I've ever seen outside my reflection in a mirror. It was your draw that brought me out of my seclusion. Pip wouldn't have been a challenge, so I let him live, hoping he'd lose that hitch in his wrist or, perhaps, get faster."

Maine extended his half-smoked cigarette toward Vermillion.

"No," said Vermillion, lifting a palm. "Thank you though."

"You seen the Swede draw?"

"Eleven?"

"That's the one."

"Nope," said Vermillion.

Maine took another pull of his cigarette, one eyebrow lifting in suggestion. "A shame that you'll never get the chance. Of the sixteen current members I've seen draw, he is the sole problem. Which reminds me…" Maine dropped the carcass of the smoldering cigarette on the ground, stamped it out. "What would you like done with your remains?"

Vermillion smiled. "It is a rare thing to see yourself in another person's words. But, even with only one eye, I see you clearly, One-Hand. Should I fall here, have me sent back to Louisville, Kentucky. There is a plot waiting for me beside a Mr. William Woodring. Winning his love was the great accomplishment of my life. My love for whiskey cost me his companionship, but not the place next to him when I die."

"What did you love about him?" asked Maine.

Vermillion's smile widened. "Only everything. He was kind. Sweet. A lover in all seasons who fell in love with a drunk. He died in '51, surrounded by his four sisters and their husbands. His mother was sick and could not be there. She died in early the next year. When I die, William will be on my right, his mother to my left."

From across the length of moonlit grass that lay between the House of the Gun and the twenty-five-maple-tree depth of the wood, raised voices muffled by the French doors and the distance found their way to the two gunfighters. "Guessing someone brought up the relationship between the Nine and Eleven," said Maine.

Vermillion did not acknowledge the interruption. "And where will I send you, Oliver? I've heard that your wife and daughter were taken from you. Will you rest next to them?"

Maine turned away from the question, looking back up into the great expanse of space to find the burning candle flame of Mars. "There are no graves for them. There will be no grave for me. The doctor advised that their bodies be burned, for the safety of those who had not become infected with the scarlet fever. I was sick and delirious when the decision was made. They were consumed by fire, so too shall I. But not tonight and not for a long while, One-Eye."

Vermillion pushed away from the trunk and

circled around to face Maine. "About that," he said, cutting a lean silhouette in the moonlight glow. "I am old, Oliver, but I am not sick. Time has stolen some of my quickness but only increased my calm. I was forty-seven when I won the One pin. Now, close to seventy, I have not drawn down on a pin in over a decade. Not because I was afraid to lose, but because I knew I would win. The competitor inside me thirsted to fight those I knew I would kill, but the man I loved and his love—the love he put inside me, Oliver—it out-leveraged the competitor." Vermillion took a step closer, the leather of his gun belt squeaking slightly. "Seeing you in Dallas, now that was something. Something I hadn't seen in a very, very long time."

Maine, unfazed by Vermillion's approach, coolly lit another cigarette with a solemn match strike. "I'm flattered," he said.

Vermillion's kindly face smoothed flat. "It isn't flattery, One-Hand. It's a warning. And the lover inside me—the old man you see before you who has lived the life you're attempting to live—is telling you, walk away. You've lived as a husband and father, a gunfighter, now I am simply saying, you may have a third life yet to live. Being the best...Oliver, being the best doesn't mean anything if it means being alone. This pin," he said, pointing at the little silver emblem pinned to his shirt lapel, "it isn't what you think it is. And because we are the people we are, it will never make you whole. The competitor can never know completion. So, take the advice of an old man: kill the competitor, resurrect your happiness."

Oliver Maine smoked and gazed into the unflinching eye of Chelsea Vermillion. "Being the best is the only happiness left for me."

His face wrinkled, kind of sad and kind of lonely. "You're wrong, Oliver. I swear to god, you're wrong."

"You know what I think?" said Maine, looking up to find Mars again, but a cloud head had rolled over, hiding the winking beacon. "I think for ten years you've been running from death, and now you see it plain as day. And like all old men who have lived at the height of it all, you are afraid to lose that. Afraid that your legacy won't be claimed by death while you are asleep. There are few more well-known legends than that of Chelsea 'Red' Vermillion, and what a catastrophe it would be for you to know that, in the end, you were not the best."

Vermillion, slow and steady, reached out to settle his hand upon Maine's shoulder. "I am the best, kid. And tonight, if you raise your challenge, I'll prove it, as I have twenty-nine times before."

"There it is," said Maine. "That's what I wanted to see."

Vermillion lifted his eyebrows, waiting.

"The sleeping gunfighter, now awake."

"You understand that every human being who has spent the sum of their life trying to reach me has never traveled beyond that point, yes? You must realize, Oliver, I am the end of you." Vermillion's voice rose, impassioned, almost pleading. "Your living, breathing end. Of all the things I have ever been named, the one I am the most, is Death's right hand."

Maine smiled that sad smile of his, all of him relaxing. "My name is Oliver Maine. I, as the Two, approach you now, Chelsea 'Red' Vermillion, as the One, amid the rules and trusts of our association that bind our fates together, and hereby challenge you officially to a contest of the gun. Legend, Death's right hand, My End, I call unto you now to yield or accept."

And Chelsea Vermillion tilted his head to the sky and let the face of the moon strike his flesh so that it burned bone white. The blue eye turned pale as the topmost spindle of a glacier. And he took in a deep breath, his next words almost a sigh. "Challenge accepted."

Vermillion walked along the space between the colonnade of trees, through the tangible radiance of the shafts of moonlight, his shoulders hunched, eyes cast low, as if he were mourning, perhaps ashamed. He set a hand smooth as alabaster upon one of the trees, high above him, where he pressed his weight into the maple, and waited.

Maine however, leaned against the silver maple tree, smoking. Calm, accomplished, certain.

After a little while, a small group of attendants dressed in black and white tuxedos came out from the House of the Gun, and in each hand they carried a white chair. Fourteen they set upon one side of the twenty-five-maple-deep row, and fourteen upon the other. With the chairs squared and set perfect as a mirror reflection, one attendant approached Vermillion. A hushed question passed between them. Vermillion nodded, saying nothing.

The attendant, hands behind his back, then approached Maine. He was young, doe-eyed, proper. "The champion has indicated that he is prepared to carry forward in the contest. As the challenger, you have the final say on if the contest goes forward."

Maine looked over to Vermillion, then back to the attendant. "My challenge remains."

"Very good, sir. For the sake of formality, I must remind you that this contest is to the death. You are both expected to fire until the other lies dead, and should one of you be wounded, the other will be expected to finish what they started. No secondary guns are allowed. If both of you fire empty, the contest shall pause and you will both be given a chance to reload. The contest will then resume with a redraw. Are the rules of the contest clear?"

"Yes," said Maine.

"Excellent. I will inform the Gold Pins." The young man smiled. "Equal luck to each of you."

A few minutes after the attendant entered the estate, the French doors of the House of the Gun opened and, spilling from the aperture, came the dangerous audience. Belle Starr, looking fierce and ravishing in the moonlight, strode at the center of the Gold Pins. To her left was Old Mute Cain and on her right walked ancient Joshua Millsap. Behind the pins gold marched the variegated motley of the pins silver. Most of them solemn, reverential. A few, craning necks to see the rows of chairs and the two gunfighters within the wood, appeared awestruck, almost disbelieving. There was one, and only one, who wore a smile: Paul Moody.

Oliver had seen Moody draw twice and been impressed not once.

The audience split where the Silver Maple Wood began, parted by the instruction of the attendant who had spoken with Maine and Vermillion. The audience, not a one of them speaking a word, were seated.

Then, the attendant went to the center of the west-facing row of chairs where the Gold Pins sat. Over his shoulder, Maine saw the eyes of

Belle Starr looking at him, eager and burning in anticipation. She spoke a word to the attendant, who straightened and took to the center of the Silver Maple Wood, now made an arena.

"Silver and Gold, Gold and Silver," said the attendant, lifting his voice to break the aching quiet. "We are come now to the end of one man or the other. Ten long years have passed since such a contest between a One and their challenger, and over twenty since this hallowed ground has been made to serve its purpose." He lifted a hand, palm up, as if serving a dinner platter. "To the east is the challenger, Oliver Maine, the Two. A man who has lived and lived and lived over the span of twenty-four contests. He is known well-over. Has proved himself as capable. And I submit him now, to you, his colleagues and rivals."

The audience clapped politely.

Maine gave them no mind.

The attendant then switched hands, the other upturned palm facing west. "And here, Gold and Silver, Silver and Gold, is the champion. For years nearly as long-numbered as the depth of the Silver Pin rank, is your unbeaten and indefatigable titan. He claimed twenty-five pins and then, with his five successful defenses, retained the One pin longer than any champion who has come before. No matter the outcome to this midnight contest, his legacy shall go on and on, for he is the only gunfighter to hold his position for near a quarter-century. Perhaps longer, perhaps no more. And so, without further ado, I submit to you, the people of the House of the Gun, your champion and the world's greatest living hazard, Chelsea Vermillion."

The crowd gave another polite applause with a single, high-pitched whistle coming from a woman Maine did not know.

When a heavy silence filled the Silver Maple Wood again, the attendant said, "Gunfighters, make your paces, and draw at the time of your choosing."

Vermillion pushed away from the tree quickly, spinning on his heel to face Maine. And the look within the pale eye of the aged gunfighter was entirely different from minutes before. His face was flush, red at the cheeks, boiling with a great anger. It was as if Vermillion had cast off the leash from some secret beast hidden within, and the color of his anger made the man look younger than his years, and very, very dangerous.

"Here," howled Vermillion, as he plodded to the center of the arena and jabbed a finger toward the ground. "Step to me, One-Hand. Now. I want them all to see." He was screaming now, a pale, wrathful god before the rest. "This is the moment you've begged life or the devil or

Death for, the moment when, with a single bullet, I transform your Two into my thirtieth."

Half the audience erupted with hoorahs and catcalls.

Maine felt sweat in his palms, but his fingers were steady. And he dipped his head, so that the brim of his hat covered his eyes and none of his smile. He sucked dead the last of his cigarette and flicked it away. Blowing out the smoke, he said, "Okay, Red," and slowly, calmly, he lifted his chin and stared into Chelsea Vermillion with the hazel, gold-rimmed eyes that had been the great love of a woman's short life, the unending color of his fatherly compassion, and the bane of every gunhand who had stood before him.

And it happened, faster than any quickdraw, Oliver Maine watched all the red rage vanish from Chelsea Vermillion's face, draining blood-less. The beast living within the veteran cham-pion showed itself to be tired, no longer thirsting, now ready to die. At the sight, Oliver Maine widened his grin and approached the One, knowing the outcome before a shot was ever fired.

When they were close enough to touch, Maine saw that Vermillion's lips were shaking, his eye wet with tears. Quietly, Vermillion said, "You have called my bluff, sir. Now, you will get the very best draw I have left within me."

Maine nodded. "You knew the outcome of

this when you saw me in Dallas. And yet still you refused to yield."

Vermillion shook his head, somber, content. "And one day, Oliver, you will understand why. Now, if you please, let me take my final paces and do what I once did best."

The men stood back-to-back. Then, they took their paces, and turned.

Oliver Maine drew fast and smooth as any gunfighter before.

Chelsea Vermillion drew slower, dying as all gunfighters dream to do: pistol in hand, falling, all battles done.

The repeat sounded the end of an old era and the beginning of the new.

CHAPTER FIVE

Le Martin-Pêcheur Hotel
New Orleans, Louisiana
March 10, 1866

Two fires burned within the walls of the grand hotel room. One, a meager flame, smoldering in the hearth. The other, an inferno, searing the collective hearts of Larry Cornish and Sven Erickson as their hands fumbled at buttons and pulled loose gun belt rigging and the shoulder sleeves of shirts, which fell to the floor like banners of longing farewell. In the wide world, the eyes and ears of so many perceived Larry as a taciturn man of slow methodologies, quick hands and quiet disposition; here, in the solitude of their finely adorned room and away from it all, did the trueness of the man reveal itself. Though Sven was larger, stronger in every way, when denuded, he was a creature of submission. For the Swede loved to be loved, to be taken care of by Larry Cornish, his greatest love. Larry, who proved deft and masterful. Insatiable. Coiling his hand around Sven's neck, Larry drew his lover into a long, deep kiss that intertwined the tapestries of their hurried hearts, weaving them all so quickly into a singular story. All their history, all that had come before the moment of their meeting less than a year ago, upon that snow-blanketed street in a nameless Kentucky town they had burned to ash, and every aching touch and every fiery kiss since, had led to this moment.

Sven, leaning to Larry's will, kissed his husband and sighed, bespelled. Happily, he gave himself over, relinquishing all his strength to Larry's want.

Larry's hands, so fast in the art of the quick-draw, never hurried, and with a bodily strength that belied the man's stature, he gripped Sven's neck tighter, drawing him down to follow. Upon a simple buffalo-hide carpet, the two men smothered one another, each happy to receive that which only the other could provide. Bodies gliding, hearts racing, Larry ran his fingers along the coils of muscle tensing along Sven's back. The touch of flesh drove both men wild, but it was the kiss they craved. Deep and sensual, their lips sank deep, deep enough to find the other's breath and the life living within them. Less than a year they had belonged to one another, and yet even from the first time, they made love as those who had made love for decades.

Delights were shared, both of them climaxing in their own time and way, but through it all, it was the kiss they came back to. Over and over, gentle and strong, shallow or deep, the kiss had always and would always be the great anchor of their unison.

"Do you remember our first time," asked Sven, laying a hand on Larry's naked thigh.

"Yes," was all Larry could say.

For just over a year, living in the aftermath glow of their love making, Larry had grown to understand a fact about himself. In the time before Sven, he'd believed in his heart, in his soul, and saw with his mind's eye, that he would only ever know contentment, never happiness. Knew with certainty that the only way life could be lived was by becoming a well-honed blade sharp enough to fend off those who despised him for what he was, and strong enough to withstand the hammer-strike blows of his enemies. It was at the age of twenty-one—eleven years before lying naked with the love of his life in the Le Martin-Pêcheur Hotel—that he saw a Silver Pin get paid exorbitantly for the simplest of jobs. And so, he went straight to the local firearms dealer and purchased the cheapest pistol and gun rig he could find. Then, smooth-faced and sweating in the afternoon heat, young and determined, he set himself within the sagging, roofless barn that was the only heirloom left to him in his father's will. He drew and drew and drew, day after day, month after month, only realizing his progress when his reflexes became faster than his decision-making.

His first official contest came six months later, when, after tracking down a woman named Alice "Big Dick" Richards, Larry found within himself the courage to challenge her: the Twenty-Five. She had laughed at him. Soberly told him, "Move on, boy. Today is not the day you have to die."

No more than three minutes later, the two squared off.

Larry's draw was so much faster that the woman froze, awestruck. And he so green, he forgot to fire. Silence filled the space between them. Slowly, carefully, she reached over, removed her pin, and tossed it to the ground. Stunned, she said, "Perhaps, today is not the day I have to die."

For the next nine years of his life, Larry found work as a guildsman, attended convocations, learned the rules, and challenged other Silver Pins. He climbed the ladder, refining himself, honing his quickdraw stroke to a beveled edge, all for the sake of becoming...becoming something the world could not deny.

And then, simply put, Sven Erickson arrived.

"You're a handsome one," Sven had said, approaching with charm and dash, no reservation.

Larry, enchanted by the man's confidence and stony gaze, opened himself to conversations he never thought he would have. Laughed and drank with him, knowing within the span of an hour that if the man asked for Larry to share his bed, there would be no denying him.

And this was the fact Larry had come to understand about himself: Sven Erickson was the world to him. He was the hand that wielded the blade Larry Cornish had become. He was, unquestionably, the unexpected happiness Larry thought would never be his.

"What do you remember about it?" asked Sven, his fingers squeezing, sometimes scratching.

Larry answered, "Everything."

Off in the distance, not more than a block away from their hotel at the midnight hour, a single pistol shot rang out. Then its repeat.

"Who do you think won?" asked Sven.

Larry turned his head, giving his eyes and heart and life to Sven all over again. "I do not care."

Sven laughed. Its sound rich, music without

lyrics. "You really are done with the Guild. After this job, I mean."

"Yes," said Larry. "We needed time. St. Guy deserves justice."

"All because you are done with the game..."

"No," said Larry. "All for the love of you."

Sven gazed into his eyes, shook his head. "I cannot believe you are in the world while I am in it. To have you is everything, Larry Cornish."

Larry slid closer, setting his cheek upon Sven's shoulder. "Everything."

"You will be careful," said Sven.

"Taking no unnecessary risk," Larry replied.

It was still dark when Larry woke. He lit a cigarette and sat at the edge of the bed, staring through the coiling smoke at the blue-black of twilight through the open window. He sat at the edge of the bed and, smoking, stared out at the moldering brick of a saloon, just visible in the window frame. Larry reached back, unlooking, and wrapped a hand around his husband's calf. Sven slept quietly, his flesh hot to the touch. Larry did not squeeze or shake to rouse him but only placed his thumb delicately upon a large vein that ran along the man's ankle. And there, in the cool quiet of that Louisiana morning, he counted the minutes of fleeting, mortal time pass in the steady, strong meter of his husband's pulse. The heartbeat that served as the metronome by which was measured the life song of Larry Cornish.

When the sun broke over the eastern stretch of the New Orleans horizon, Larry was fully dressed and Sven, one leg hanging over the bed where he lay, appraised him. "One more roll in the hay before you go?"

Larry's footfalls sounded so heavy in his own ears as he approached. He sat upon the bed, all the while looking into Sven's eyes. A man of few words and little mirth, save for what Sven had unearthed within him, he placed his hand upon Sven's, patted once. Twice.

A third time.

"I will be okay," said Sven, knowing Larry's mind. "Whatever comes of this 'Falconer's' contract. You'll be okay on your little fox hunt, too."

Larry looked away, eyes finding the red dawn, blue sky, and the pink clouds purpling at the reach of the horizon. "Telegram."

Sven reached up and glided a finger along Larry's jaw, turning the man's eyes back to him. "Often as I can."

Larry's eyes flicked down, then back to Sven's. In those transfixing orbs, he saw color and light and the vast sprawl of all the teeming life inside the man he loved. "Be fast. Accurate. Safe," he said.

Sven smiled big. "Only if you do the same." He leaned forward, kissed his husband once more. "Go on now, Nine. Show the Queen of all those soiled doves that while we may be coming to the end of the age of gunfighters, it has saved its best for last."

Friends and Lovers

ABOARD THE STEAM TRAIN *HEPHAESTUS*, EN ROUTE FROM SAVANNAH, GEORGIA, TO CHARLOTTE, NORTH CAROLINA MARCH 12, 1866

M aster,

Were it not for the rolling wheels of the train you gifted or the choir of dark angels filling my dreams, I would sleep. The train wheels are only a small annoyance. I find myself getting used to their locomotive percussion. The engineer you provided calls it 'the churn.' I think he has the right of it. But it is not the churn that keeps my mind swirling with activity. Nothing about the steady, pounding thrum toward our mission unsettles my thoughts, not really. I believe I only mentioned it as a way to speak about the latter subject of my first sentence.

When I close my eyes, I hear a song. A melody that feels intimate and old. Older than I. Older than Man. Old as all and greater than all else. There are...

voices...that sing with sounds that cannot be words, for they follow no meter of syllabic understanding. Somehow, though my ears cannot compile the meaning, I feel their intent. The words are ancient, secret, filling me as headwaters feed a river. My eyes are heavy, tired, lacking acuity. My heart is heavy, too, as if tied to a great stone and dropped into the deepmost sea. And my mind...my thoughts...plagued by the choir-sound, stretch to void, as if I have been brought to the center of the universe—no...no...as if I have been made the center of the universe. Set as its axis. All that exists, spindled atop the pinpoint of me.

Was this what you meant when you set your promise upon my heart?

Is this the burden of fulfillment? To see at such distance. To hear the hymn that shall unlock the binding cable of all things. To feel...to feel this way, sobered by the all that you have professed to me— your servant. The weight drains my faculties. But do not dismay, this is not a testimony letter of what I am unable to endure. Rather it is my confession to my High Priest; the weariness inside me is only a testament to my dedication to you, my Ebenezer stone. You who elected me long before I knew that election was mine to have. You, who looked upon the innumerable faces set upon the world stage with keen eye and steady heart and decided that it was I who should make the way for the Nine.

The churn of the Hephaestus *drives us toward Charlotte. I have been there once before, as a little girl, where I fell in love with the tulip trees and oaks and sentinel sweetgums. And it seems fated now that, having once before seen the vast mining operation where so much of father's wealth was unearthed, I, as your instrument, am guided back to the copper veins of Rudisill Lode. Those shining streams will lead me to the object of our requirement. I am sure of it. In my restlessness I have remained vigilant in my bird watching. I have seen cardinal and blue jay and many a crow, but there has been no falcon sign. Though I must admit, only two days ago, I called upon my soldiers to flay a man I suspected to be a spy or messenger of our enemies. Though he admitted to numerous sins and begged for death many, many times, had he been an enemy, I would have extracted his falcon song. A mistake in overzealous caution. I only make mention of the event in the chance that the body somehow rises from the river where we laid it over with many heavy stones. If circumstance brings that to bear, the desquamated state we left the body in will certainly draw the attention of the Georgia newspapers. If these actions displease you, do not think them rash or hazardous to our cause, but trust in me, High Priest. Trust that all I have done and am doing is for you...for us...our mission.*

And it is that mission which compels me. The right truthfulness of it. The cold reality of its impor-tance. You, the bright star of my revelation, pulled back the curtain of human primacy to illuminate. The fire of you burned away all shadow of delusion and self-conceit and ignorance which concealed those those raging, beautiful titans who, once I recover the gatestone, will once again reign. This time forever. I swear I will. I swear to you and to the members of our society that I am all that you believe me to be.

The strong right arm of Prometheus. Hand-maiden of the Nine. And forever,

Your baroness,

Gwendolyn Pierce Butler

CHAPTER SEVEN

ABOARD THE TRAIN
PURPLE MARTIN LIMITED,
EN ROUTE FROM NEW ORLEANS
TO SAVANNAH, GEORGIA
MARCH 15, 1866

Sven Erickson sat in the diner car of the *Purple Martin Limited*, drinking his coffee, waiting on his breakfast while people streamed past him in the hurry and bustle of off-loading or boarding the train. Despite having left the House of the Gun with Judge Hezekiah Ellison, it had been a lonely trip. The patron had not said much while they traveled to the New Orleans rail yard to make their way toward the East Coast. And when Sven pressed the man for more information about the purpose of their mission, he'd only said, "My mind is preoccupied with the letters I need to write, Mr. Erickson. You have my word: once they are drafted, we will talk more. Our full company awaits us in Savannah. Likely you will know more then. How much more...I have not yet determined."

Sven had only nodded, watching Midnight get loaded into the stable car. He was not a man of letters so he had not known what time frame to expect, yet he was still surprised when the Judge spent not hours but whole days in his room.

Whenever the Judge did emerge from his room, which was down the narrow hall of the red-carpeted passenger car, he seemed always in deep thought, spoke to no one, and dined quickly and alone. During the four-day journey from New Orleans to Savannah, Sven preoccupied himself with a novel entitled *War and Peace*. It was fine enough, with one particular section that caught him by the heart, reminding him of Larry. He memorized it, held it close, waited to share. Most of the rest of the book was fine, but he found his concentration broken over and over by the splendor of America rolling by and thoughts of Larry Cornish within him. At two stops, one in Mississippi and the other just at the Georgia/Alabama border, he kept his promise, sending telegrams to Larry, both of them saying simply:

All well.
   All of my love,

- Your Eleven.

Sven looked out the window of the diner car. It was a fine, cool morning, a choppy sea of clouds rolling unto the stretch of everything, no blue to be seen. The Central Junction rail station was two stories of red brick and white-framed windows looking stately in the early morning light. The eight o'clock hour was a full rush for the place with women and men, children, all of them dressed fancy, hands full, ready for long journeys and perhaps new beginnings. One boy, no older than twelve and wearing a hat three sizes too big, hooked his little fingers into the large, pockets of his hand-me-down trousers and turned his head from side to side, appraising the whole damn train like he owned the thing. And then, much to Sven's delight, the boy forced the entire line of boarding passengers to wait a moment while he stopped, gave his eyes to a pretty teenage girl, tipped his hat and with all the confidence the world will afford such a child, he said, "Howdy, ma'am."

Sven smiled over the lip of his coffee cup, whispering too low for the boy to hear, "Go ahead, young man. Go ahead."

Finally, pushed along by a smirking, proud father, the little Casanova and the rest of the passenger line rolled through to have their tickets punched and to settle inside. Just as Sven had settled back into reading the novel, a big hand clapped down on his shoulder.

"Morning, Erickson," said the Judge, and then settled his great bulk into the chair opposite. He looked out the window toward the Central Junction landing, scratched that big, black beard of his. "Ah, I see my people readying to board."

Sven looked out the window, saw a line of latecomers, all standing there waiting for admittance. "Which ones?"

"Tall fella there, one with the fancy suit and hat that looks like a chamber pot, and the woman next to him. Professor Robert Bass and Sarah Lockhart." He shifted, smoothed a wrinkle out of his shirt, somehow seeming evasive. "To make it clear, these are my people, Mr. Erickson, and I trust them with almost everything, but the orders come from me. If there is a decision to be made, I may inquire as to my friends' opinions on the matter, but ultimately, there will never be a vote. I run the outfit." A little smile slashed through his beard. "Sarah is a woman on fire and prone to violence, which I am sure you appreciate. She talks like she runs the whole damn world—and she may do that one day— however, her word does not circumvent mine. Bass is an eccentric, but we've known each other a long time. He is an energetic mind, a question machine, but in the end, he never questions me."

"You're the patron," said Sven. "My action belongs to you so long as you don't ask me to do the things I've stated I will not do."

Ellison nodded. "Good. Also, I appreciate you being cordial at my seclusion. There are many fronts upon which my agents are engaged." The man smeared his fingers across his tired face. "Seeing the whole conflict requires all of me. Now that my correspondences and telegrams have been sent, my whole focus is here. Now."

Sven gave a little smile. Saying nothing, only sipping his coffee and waiting.

Professor Bass and Sarah Lockhart strolled onto the train, him ahead of her, and came down the aisle, each with a bag in hand. The Judge stood up to greet them. Sven remained seated.

"Robert," said the Judge, shaking the slender man's wiry hand.

"My friend," he replied, jovial, energetic.

The woman gave what might have been the most unashamed smile Sven had ever seen, brandishing its stark whiteness the way a gunfighter spins a pistol in flourish.

The Judge opened his arms and hugged her.

"Hey there, gorgeous," she said.

"Hey yourself, kid," said the Judge.

Sarah Lockhart looked over the Judge's shoulder at Sven with eyes the color of dew-soaked hazelnuts. Those eyes struck him hard, revealing the edge of her sharp appraisal. "New friend?"

"Yes, yes," said the Judge, turning back. "This is—"

"My name is Sven Erickson," he said, and as he rose, he brought to bear all his height and charm, throwing his own smile back at her. "It is my pleasure to meet you, Ms. Lockhart. And you, Mr. Bass."

"My, my," said Sarah. "I don't know what accent that is, but I wonder if they grow them all as big as you wherever you're from."

"Dutch," said Professor Bass. "Yes?"

"You have a good ear," said Sven. Then he looked back to Sarah. "I have a brother and a sister back home, both no bigger than you. My father, a horrible man, called them his pride and joy. Me, he called 'the ox that refuses to pull the plow.' My size, like much of me, is uncommon."

"Good in a brawl, I bet," said Sarah, playful.

"Fair in a brawl. In a gunfight, the best."

The Judge nodded. "Mr. Erickson here is a shootist of the highest order. He's just signed on with us."

"For the money or the mission?" asked Bass.

"Neither," said Sven. "But for the only reason that really matters: my husband told me to."

Sarah and Bass both laughed. The Judge, however, extended his hand to gesture toward the passenger-car door just beyond them. "Mission is something we need to discuss immediately. Come, join me."

Sven followed the Judge and his agents out the diner car, through several passenger cars, every seat full, a little bar, a barbershop attended by a skinny woman cutting the hair of a silver-haired gambler who was yammering on about some poker tournament he won on a fancy Louisiana riverboat the moment they walked in and would likely keep telling the tale until the end of time. The barber smiled and nodded at Sven. A silent invitation to come back should he require her services.

The caboose was the *Purple Martin Limited*'s drawing room. It was pure opulence with lush red carpet, windows running from chair rail to ceiling, and gold curtains sinched by white tassels and fastened in mother of pearl. All the trim was polished brass.

"Sit," said the Judge, pointing dismissively at four deep leather chairs set two-by-two. "I need to tell you—"

"Before you start," said Professor Bass, ignoring the Judge's request to walk over to the self-service bar, "I have some news." He poured himself a healthy portion from a crystal decanter filled to the neck with whiskey. "I need you to know that Pepper Johnson is dead."

The Judge, who had appeared to Sven as

strong and confident and emotionally immove-able in his demeanor, slumped at the shoulders and sagged at the knees until he settled into the chair beneath him.

Bass garnished his drink with bitters, saying nothing.

Sarah Lockhart took off her hat, somber. The look on her face was so sincere, so wounded, that the pain she felt reached across the distance between them and touched Sven, making him sad too.

"He was tracking the *Hephaestus*," said the Judge, his voice as diminished as the man who owned it. "What about Billy?"

Bass took a sip of his whiskey. "Billy is alive. Sent word to me just yesterday. Pepper was watching the movements of the Society's new woman; apparently, he followed too close in too thin a crowd. Looked too long. She caught wind of him and had her men take him at gunpoint. Other details are sparse, questions abound, but..." The Professor's eyes looked into the whiskey glass in his hand, found a distance there before he drained it dry. Then, with a hard, final swallow, he said, "They flayed him alive. Starting with the feet, all the way to the shoulders, Hezekiah."

"Goddamn," said Sven, the word leaking out of him as he envisioned such torture.

"He did not give us up," said Bass. "He remained true."

In the silence, there came the steady growth of breathing, louder and louder, from the Judge. In through the nose, whistling out through the mouth. Like the *Purple Martin Limited* building its steam to roll its way out of Savannah, the Judge boiled hot, the anger inside all too clear. His eyes hardened to stones in the chiseled features of his reddening face.

Neither Sarah or the Professor said anything, but both watched him, tears in their eyes.

Bass walked back over to the Judge and placed a hand on his shoulder. "I know this distresses you, Hez—"

"I, uh..." He sucked his teeth, shook his head. "I will send Jessica a letter. Make sure she and their boy...T-taylor?"

"Travis," said Bass. "His boy is Travis."

The Judge nodded. "Make sure they get his wages." He then gave Bass a sharp look. "Where is Billy now?"

"Still following," said Bass. "Keeping his distance. But the manifest for the train is listed for Charlotte, which confirms my suspicions and means we are on the right path."

"They must be searching for the manuscript?"

Bass swallowed. "No," he said, flicking his eyes to Sven and then to Sarah, concerned.

"Remember, we intercepted the telegram at the Pennsylvania exchange. Barron acquired the manuscript months ago."

"Right," said the Judge, looking tired, faculties diminished. "One of the obelisks then."

"Yes," said Sarah, then paused patiently, as if giving her patron a moment to breathe. Collect his thoughts. "The Professor believes that the Society has found one of the summoning sites. Whoever is guiding their actions has dispatched this woman to find it."

Ellison fingered his way into his coat and from his breast pocket produced a smoking pipe with a fat, acorn-shaped bowl. He popped the stem into his mouth, struck a match on a boot heel, brought the vessel to life. After a few almost alarmingly deep draws on the pipe, his eyes flared with their previous intensity. "What do we know of her, this new woman?"

"Almost nothing," said Bass, walking back over to the little bar. He refilled his glass with another long pour. "Only that she is referred to by her men as 'Baroness.'"

Sven shook his head. "Baroness of what? This society?"

Everyone turned, stared at him. Then the agents looked to the Judge, waiting.

Ellison drew deeply on his pipe, considered for a time, then nodded. "Mr. Erickson, what I am going to tell you comes in the strictest of confidence. If it must leave this room, it can never venture beyond the circle of people here within it. Is that clear?"

"You're the billfold. You decide."

Ellison narrowed his eyes. "Say that you understand and will comply."

"Sure," he said.

Just visible behind the curtain of smoke shrouding the Judge's face burned the full measure of his penetrating intelligence, examining Sven, looking old and weathered, careful, discerning. "You cannot understand our enemies until you understand our work, Mr. Erickson. And the work of the Peregrine Estate is a labor of love: love for all humankind. I began this labor with my sister over thirty years ago and dedicated my life, my sanity, and all my earthly wealth to the belief that every single person is worthy of protection. No matter their birthplace or who they were in the time before their now. Every human being is worth hoping for. All of us. My life, my work, they are set within that unassailable Rock of Ages: the inalienable dignity vested inside the wellspring of every human heart. The peregrine falcon is our sign, for it is swift, territorial, and it soars highest just before it takes the plunge to strike." His eyes never left Sven's as he spoke. His voice so quiet, filled with the unmistakable zeal of the true believer. "There are those who have been poisoned by greed and hate, who despise the very species to which they belong. I know this, because I was once one of them."

"What changed?" said Sven, drawn in by the old man's...was this a confession?

"Simple," said Ellison, a sad smile forming on his lips, which trembled for a second and no more. "Love came into my life."

Sven was struck by the sheer sincerity of the statement, its uncomplicated truth. And, he realized that the same had happened for him: the world had been one thing until Larry Cornish arrived, and all too quickly he made the world all together something else.

Sarah smiled.

Bass lifted an eyebrow, holding back a grin.

"Through my sister and her unrelenting love for me," the Judge continued, "I realized that though I had been raised among people whose only passion is the enfeeblement of all humanity has come to cherish and hold and find worth living for, they did not get to decide who I was. Who I could become. They are known as the Society of Prometheus. They worship a pantheon of gods they believe once ruled over man in what they call 'the Time Before.' Their beliefs come from an ancient, malevolent tome. Only certain individuals can read this manuscript, and the process of learning the old language holds a cost few can bear. They are a plague, hoping to unmake all that we have built by summoning their gods back unto our world."

Sven didn't believe in gods, or in any supernatural beings for that matter, and yet something in the way the Judge spoke was filling him with unease. It was as if the man's beliefs were seeping into him, his words filling up the fissures of uncertainty that exist inside atheist and believer alike. It was because of their certainty, and the temerity in his voice, that the mountain holdfast of spiritual dismissal walling Sven's heart opened its doors to let this man, this stranger, inside. Ellison's words, the truth living in the wind of them, shattered Sven's surety of self. Made him question.

"You expect me to believe that?"

The Judge leaned his head to one side, looking almost longingly to the window where the red-gold sunlight falling across Savannah bounced off its buildings and fields and reflected in through the window, casting his skin in golden blush tones. "It is a hard thing to explain," he said. "The only way to prove their belief would be to allow them to succeed. But I have witnessed the effect the manuscript has on those who read it, and that alone has made me a believer. What is written upon those pages in the tolling language drives the reader mad, tears a person apart from heart to soul." He looked back to Sven, his eyes cold, serious. "And if that's what the words alone do, I am arrested by what their deeper rituals might portend. I am not a man given over to terror, but..." The Judge swallowed hard. "When it comes to the Society of Prometheus, and learning of their designs, it is the only appropriate response."

"It's all real," said Sarah Lockhart. "Real as you and me, this train, the ground we're rolling on. It's real."

"They speak true," said Professor Bass. "A lesser skeptic would deride their claims. Call them lunatics and puppets of superstition. A lesser skeptic would not have investigated these claims as deeply, questioned as dispassionately, or probed and examined so thoroughly; but I am not a lesser skeptic, Mr. Erickson. I am a man of science, of logic. Reason and measurement of things previously unseen. When I joined the Peregrine Estate, I did so as—and I hate to use a *religious* metaphor—as Saul did on his way to Damascus. Learning the truth of these people and their aims threw the scales from my eyes, giving me greater vision. A clarity to the questions I had otherwise refused to ask. The Judge uses his passion to recruit. Sarah her rage to do justice. And I my questions, to find truth. One question I shall not ever allow to be answered is thus: What will happen to the world if the Society of Prometheus achieves their goals?"

Sven shook his head, trying to understand.

"You've already purchased me from the Guild, and you have my gun for so long as this mission requires. But I don't have to believe in what you do to kill or protect as you see fit. Why the hard sell?"

Ellison drew on his pipe once again, then said, "Because once you see, nothing will be the same, and it would be unfair of me not to forewarn you. Your life will change, Mr. Erickson. Once we arrive in Charlotte and find this Baroness, there will be a moment when your eyes and ears will seem to deceive you. Where the bedrock of your understanding will shake. When that happens, look to me. Or to the Professor or to Sarah. Let our experience help your steadfastness. Lean on our resolve."

There was the familiar notion within Sven to throw out a charming jape or confident declaration, but he found nothing within himself to say. He only considered deeply, then looked them over one by one, and said, "I will."

CHAPTER EIGHT

ABOARD THE STEAMER
RED RIVER KING
NATCHEZ, MISSISSIPPI
MARCH 16, 1866

L arry Cornish sat in his cabin aboard the *Red River King,* watching the muddy waters of the Mississippi ripple, swirl, churn beneath the steamer. The sun was set low in a ruddy, cloudless sky, its light scattered all through the dense foliage of oak and sweetgums lining the river, as if someone had fired a shotgun shell through the portrait of the world. Next to the him, on a little bedside table, a cigarette burned. A single coil of slender smoke drifted from the ember of the cylinder, filling the cabin with a scent that sometimes smelled like sugar fudge, other times unmistakably maple. Larry had taken an ounce of Sven's tobacco while he slept in their hotel bed. He had placed it in a leather pouch for safekeeping, and for when he wanted to remember. Sven was a prodigal consumer, full of mirth, rarely taking the time to measure what he had, knowing that if there was too little he would simply acquire more. Larry, having lived hard and lean his whole life before Sven, had taken only an ounce, never wanting to take too much. But he had taken it all the same, unapologetically and without mention. Sven would not miss the ounce, but Larry would miss Sven a little less by having it. The scent made him grin a little grin as he stared out over the water, the spaces between the dense foliage and morning sunlight glorifying them both.

A knock came at the cabin door. Larry, gazing outside and unmoving, said, "Yes?"

"Captain says we're near Natchez. Unloading before midday. Horner wants all of us to break-fast together. So, if you are so inclined, Nine."

Larry's clenched his jaw. "Will be with you presently."

"Mr. Horner will be glad of it," said Moody, his voice muffled by the door, the smartass smile in his tone easily coming through. "He believes you are too love sick to be useful."

At that, Larry slowly turned his head and looked back at the door, his heartbeat skipping to a more angry speed. He said nothing, glaring at the peephole as if it were Moody's eye.

Another moment passed. "We'll save you a seat." The thumping of Moody's sauntering gait came abruptly, then faded so that Larry Cornish was left with only the smoldering cigarette, the Louisiana morning, and the bitterness of life among enemies. With two spit-wetted fingers, he quickly pinched the ember of the cigarette, snuffing the flame to save what he could for later. And, putting on his hat and cinching himself at the waist with his gunbelt, Larry told himself that even without Sven there, he was a whole man. Capable, dangerous, and worth fearing.

He made his way out of the cabin and into the mild and breezy air, rubbing his fingertips together and then squeezing them into fists. Down the stairs, just past the hurricane deck of the strolling *Red River King*, there was a grand saloon where stood Paul Moody and Michael Horner at the end of a short line, waiting for a table. When Horner saw Larry take the last stair onto the main deck, he appraised Larry with those pale, limestone eyes, readying a jape. Larry approached slow, like a man with all the time in the world to get to where he was going.

"Well, Larry Cornish," Horner began, "the Nine himself graces us with—"

Now within reaching distance, Larry moved smooth and fast, sliding up close and slapping the palm of his left hand down on the butt of Horner's pistol, pinning it there. Horner, shocked, reached for Larry's hand, but stopped when Larry's drawn revolver pressed itself deep into the flesh beneath his chin.

"What the fu—"

The man in front of Horner, perhaps younger than a hundred years, lifted the thousand cracked wrinkles of his weather-beaten face so wide that the blue of his eyes could be seen as they had once been in his youth.

"Do I appear useful," said Larry, flat and cold.

"You can't—" Horner made a choking sound as Larry shoved the barrel of his pistol harder up into his chin.

Larry ratchetted back the hammer. "Do I," he repeated, very slowly, "appear useful."

Horner turned his head to look at Moody, the eyes of a man half afraid and wholly betrayed. "You told him?"

Moody shook his head, laughing that laugh of his. It was a sound that came through his teeth, more a hiss than a whistle, snake-like. "Thought it would be funny to see Larry angry. And to confirm what I only previously suspected."

Larry looked back, just over the hump of his shoulder, said to Moody, "Suspected what?"

"You're faster when you're angry, Nine. A rarity."

Larry took a deep breath, slowly uncocked the hammer of his revolver, and looked hard into the eyes of Michael Horner. "I will not be defamed."

Horner, youngest among the three gunfighters by a decade or more, rubbed a palm over the flesh of his chin as if trying to smooth away the embarrassment and the little hurt the gun barrel had made.

The old man standing ahead of him in the breakfast line shook his head, disappointed. "You goddamn Silver Pins," he said with the authority of the wise. "You run so hot-blooded and carefree. Pullin' your fucking pistols like we aren't a civilization with law and order. Goddamn, derelicts...all of you goddamn derelicts of character."

Horner leveled his shoulders and opened his mouth, likely to cuss back at the old man, but Moody put up two fingers and silently glared at him. Horner's eyes flared, then his mouth closed.

A few minutes later, the three were sitting at a little table in the corner of the grand saloon. The *Red River King*'s captain—or designer or decorator; Larry did not know who made such decisions in the adornment of a steamboat—had truly leaned into the color in the name. With its scarlet carpet, matching curtains, and a lacquered bar set before a ten-foot painting of Texas's Red River, the whole of the saloon was bright and filled with life. To the left of the bar and a lovely bay window latticed in a red frame, a band composed of a guitar man and violist played a quiet but lively tune. The concavity of the bay window magnified the morning sunlight, giving the players an almost ethereal quality. Opposite the musician was a buffet piled high with biscuits and peppered sausage gravy, pancakes, and sterling serving cylinders pearled over by dark beads of molasses, perhaps spilled by an overzealous child.

The Silver Pins ate, drank lots of hot, black coffee, said nothing until they were done.

"You ever been to Natchez?" asked Horner to Moody, leaning back in his chair satisfied.

"Nope," said Moody.

"Cornish?"

"A time or two," said Larry over the lip of his mug.

"Before I was a Pin, I ran with a little gang in Natchez..." Horner took a deep breath, readying a story.

Moody sighed, interrupting. "No one gives a shit, Twelve."

Horner screwed up his face, his voice dipping low, angry: "You know, I heard you were unpleasant."

""I don't want to hear about your life or your—"

"Don't speak for all of us," said Larry, giving Moody a cold look.

Moody sniffed a laugh. "Larry Cornish, connoisseur of middling raconteurs."

"Horner knows the city. You should listen."

Horner smirked. "Yeah, Eight. I know Natchez *and* Natchez Under-the-Hill. Spent a year there running with an outfit named—"

"Will this story provide me with greater understanding of how to find the men we are hunting?" asked Moody, though he was looking at Larry, his gaze unwavering.

"I was just making conversation goddamnit…," said Horner.

"I didn't think so." Moody picked up a silk, scarlet napkin, dabbed at the corners of his mouth. "It is simple. We will visit the brothel, question the paramours, ascertain if these men have visited again, and discover where they are residing. How's that?"

"Straightforward," said Larry.

"Easiest guild job in the history of guilds or jobs," said Moody, tossing his napkin onto the table. "Listen, I didn't sit down here to talk about finding the morons who hurt Reine Silvia's favorite little bird, and I didn't throw my hat into the ring out of some idealistic notion that hurting these guys will somehow give St. Guy justice. His face is fucked—fucked forever—and killing those that done it won't change a thing about that stone-cold fact. No, I signed on for two reasons: money," he said, and then pointed a lazy finger at Larry, "and you."

"Me," said Larry.

"Absolutely."

"Why?"

Moody sneered, settled back lazily into his chair. "I've seen near every gunfighter the Guild has to offer, Cornish. Seen you. Seen Horner, who we both know is a dead man walking if he challenges the Eleven. And I have seen your lover, who is in fact the point: Erickson was storming right up the ranks toward me. Oh, you were making your way along too. Take no insult—not at that. Not yet. See, I was waiting for him to make it to me, because he is one of the only two living pistoleers who makes me nervous."

"The other being Oliver Maine," said Horner, jumping in.

Moody looked at him dismissively, insulted at the interruption. "If you talk again, I will kill you where you sit. So, unless you're ready to take a deep fucking breath through the middle of your forehead, I suggest you heed. Now, as I was—"

"Fuck you, Moody," said Horner, his words rushed, filled with the fiery temper and invincibility of youth. The words were so loud that half the saloon turned to look at their table.

There was no hesitation. Paul Moody's

sitting draw was quick, effortless. Fast as they come. The easy motion of a natural whose innate talent makes him uncatchable to even the most stalwart practitioner. He knew it, too. The satisfied smirk on his face exemplified the gunfighter; nothing made this man happier than to simply be given a reason to exercise his killing technique. The hammer drew back, click-click-click in the middle of the draw, and the nickel–plated barrel caught the sheen of scarlet sunlight burning through the curtains to shade the pistol in the dominating color of the *Red River King*.

"Challenge," said Larry, faster than Moody's trigger finger.

Horner sucked in a breath, his hands so much slower than Moody's that his palms had only just left the table where they rested.

Moody, pistol aimed at Horner, turned his head slowly to look at Larry. Smirk still on his face. "Look at you," he said. "Quick to speak. Pity your hands are so slow."

Horner, staring into the empty, zero-shaped void of the pistol, blew out the breath.

Heart racing, Larry's fingers ached to reach for the gun at his side. To feel the smoothness of the sandalwood grip, the weight of the draw, and the faster-than-a-blink stroke that had been his stock and trade for many years. But he was a man of slow methods, and outside his soul's burning desire to love and be loved by Sven, he was also a creature of calculation. A man who had honed himself like he had refined his draw: the greatest efficiency delivering the greatest effect.

"You're challenging me?" asked Moody, a little disbelief in his voice. "Right here? Now?"

"Yield or accept," said Larry, unwavering.

Moody squinted, then his eyes relaxed. "Guild rules dictate that we cannot duel while hired on by the same patron for the same purpose."

"Correct."

"So, you're challenging me to a duel you know I must wait to fight, all for the sake of this...this *gunfighter* who will never rise higher than where he currently rests?"

"By the rules of our mutual association, Paul Moody, accept," said Larry, "or yield."

Moody's smirk split at the lips to reveal his straight, white teeth. His shoulders shook as he began chuckle, and then to laugh. He looked to Horner, laughing, shoulders bouncing, as if he was amusement incarnate. And with a swift flourish of his pistol, spinning it backward once and uncocking the hammer in the flow, he holstered the gun. "Hahaha, hell yes. I, the Eight, accept your challenge, Nine. You may be a goddamn sexual profligate, but fuck me if your balls aren't made of brass." Then, laughing all the while and pleased as a killer can be, he stood up from his chair. "Soon," he said to Larry. "Real soon." And then made his exit.

The eyes within the saloon had followed Moody and were no longer on the two gunfighters at the table.

"First you threaten to kill me in public for insulting you behind your back," said Horner, "then you save my life."

"Was angry. Had no intent to fire," said Larry. "It was imprudent of me to draw on you like I did."

Horner smirked a bit, perhaps feeling better because of Larry's apology. But then a realization, acting as a thief, stole the smirk. "Moody would have."

"He is right," said Larry. "You are the Twelve. Attempt to climb higher, and it will mean your grave."

The young gunfighter's face slumped to a frown, masking him in offense. "You've never seen me draw, Nine."

"You, no. Sven, yes."

Horner grit his teeth, his hands balling into fists. "I'll get faster."

"Your temper will kill you first," said Larry. "Would have today if not for me."

At that, Horner seemed to relax, drawn back into what had just transpired. "Moody is fast. Maybe fast as Maine. And you challenged him."

"Yes."

"Do you think you can win? Beat him at twenty-five paces."

Larry looked to the scarlet curtains, chewed his cheek, considering.

"Well?"

"At my best, he at his... no," said Larry.

"You set the challenge, knowing you'd lose?"

"Tertiary concern. Saved your life. Increased the possibility of job success for Reine Silvia. Worth the risk."

Horner appraised him, shaking his head. "You are a strange one, Nine."

"To all but one," he said, and, wanting no more the company of gunfighters or eaters or anyone in the goddamn world who wasn't Sven Erickson, Larry got up from the table without another word and went back to his cabin.

Once inside, he locked the door, then went over to the bedside table. He picked up the pinched cigarette, which felt dry and brittle in his fingers. He lit it once again, took a single pull to bring it to smoldering life, but did not inhale. Setting the cigarette back down, Larry then settled himself into his chair and returned his quiet appraisal to the river. The tobacco smoke coiled all through the air, returning the scent and the memories too. He watched as the afternoon sun burnished the muddy Mississippi waters, kept watching until it was directly above them, high in the air so that it made the little ripples shine bright as crystal.

With a shriek from its steam whistle, the *Red River King* split all sound, and after its shrill cry, a man could be heard outside. "Natchez! Offloading for Natchez! Fifteen minutes to Natchez!"

Charlotte, North Carolina
March 18, 1866

Sven Erickson rode, accompanied by a judge, a professor, and a thunderstorm disguised as a woman, through a tall grass glade sloping to valley. He kept Midnight at a steady trot, matching the pace of the others.

"You know, I have been here before," said Professor Bass, riding a painted bay he called Little Brown, for she was mostly white. "A few years before the war, a prospector friend of mine brought me along this very trail. This valley we're in, he told me, was once claimed by a Frenchman who had left Paris because a woman declined his marriage proposal. So, heartbroken, pockets full of his aristocrat father's money, he came here and made a claim of land. He named it

La Vallée du Cœur en Deuil, which of course means—"

"Robert," said the Judge, slapping the flat of his palm on his neck to kill a mosquito. "I think you are wonderful and deeply enjoy your ability to bring the history of a place to life, but—"

"Well, I just believe in the importance of being an informed traveler," said Bass, who then took a deep breath, reloading his lungs for another verbal salvo.

"Professor," said Sarah. "What the Judge is trying to say is—"

"Ms. Lockhart, do you think I do not know the polite wind-up of a man who will, soon after I refuse to stop talking because it is the way I pass the time, brazenly tell me to shut the fuck up?"

Sven chuckled, riding along, last in the pack. He'd been on lots of jobs as a hired gun but never had his patrons been this...well, the only word was 'connected.'

Bass turned back, having heard the laugh. "You see how they treat me, Mr. Erickson? I regale them with North Carolina history, ecology. Stories of a land they have never known!"

The Judge swatted another bug, smearing the blood it had stolen upon his neck. "This is my fifth time in this state, Robert. Likely the last time I visit it with you."

Sven outright laughed, leaning forward at the waist to come near Midnight's neck.

"Oh, even the hired gun laughs at my expense," said Bass, over-performing his offense. "My word, what is the world coming to when the populous surrounding an educated man refuse to allow him to speak. To illuminate. To question!"

"Robert," said the Judge, slanting a grin at his friend.

Professor Bass, with a big smile and eyes wide as a child who is about to be given a gift, looked back to Sven. "Here it comes…"

The Judge, laughing for the first time since he'd received news of his agent's brutal demise, said, "Shut the fuck up."

Their laughter rolled through the glade, along the broken-crystal shine of the shallow, rocky stream in the center of the valley. The slopes were carpeted with blooming wildflowers and trees Sven did not know, all leafed out, catching the sun. It was as pretty as spring can make a day. And it happened so quickly, swift as the wind changing, Sven wished Larry was here. Longed to see if his husband's rare smile would have peeked out at the company's teasing of each other. More likely, Larry would have cocked an eyebrow at the whole thing, silently musing thoughts he would never say.

"Mr. Erickson," said Sarah Lockhart, drawing

closer. Her stout quarter horse, Sisqo, did not seem to care for the unsteady, rocky terrain near the streambed. "Can I ask you a personal question?"

"If it will keep all of you from further deriding the Professor," said Sven, jokingly taking a side.

"Aha!" proclaimed Bass, as if winning a great victory. "This man understands."

"—and also serve the purpose of silencing him," said Sven.

Bass slumped at the shoulders, playing it up. "This man understands nothing and has made himself my mortal enemy."

Sarah ignored him. "Do you happen to know Oliver Maine?"

"I know *of* Maine. He fought for the One position just last week in a midnight duel at the House of the Gun."

Sarah brought Sisqo to a stop, bringing the horse's broadside to face Sven. When he said nothing, she shot him a look. "And?"

"And what? "Did you know him?"

"Did?" Her smile vanished, and her face grew serious, concerned. ""Did he not survive?"

"Ms. Lockhart, if you know Maine and have seen him draw, then you already know the answer to your question."

She rolled her eyes up to the sky in thanks, elation masking her face. "So, he won."

"Yes. And from what I hear in spectacular fashion, making it look easy."

Her eyebrows rose and she gave a crooked smile, remembering. "He does do that. So, that means he is the One Pin, yes?"

Sven smirked. "For now," was all he said.

Sarah glowered darkly at him.

He was gathering that this was a person whose emotions were set on a pendulum, swaying back and forth, back and forth. A woman unable to experience the middle space between feelings, only the highest heights and the deepest depths. And that realization made Sven only like Sarah more, because he was the exact same way.

They rode along the little stream which widened and deepened as they traveled. The trail widened too, becoming more like a road where it intersected with a more well-trod path.

"West leads back to Charlotte," said the Professor, pointing to his left. And with a flick of his wrist, he swapped the direction. "East leads to, well," he mused, "who can say what lays in wait for us?"

"Existentially, sure," said the Judge. "But the mine is that way, correct?"

"Rudely, Hezekiah, yes."

The sun climbed high, shining hot and bright. It somehow found every gap within the skyflung field of cottony clouds, its heat lathering the horses in sweat, and the Judge's agents too. The road rose so sharply that each mount walked at a tilt, straining all the way up, and then sloped hard on the descent, so that each horse went heavy on their forehand, near uncollected, on the way down. But each rider showed their skill, taking their time with great care. Then, at an unmarked turnoff, Professor Bass directed the group into a hardwood thicket dominated by red maples. They stretched over the road, forming a shadowy tunnel that wound so sharp only the bend could be seen.

"We're close," said Bass, his voice absent of its usual jovial tone.

"Good," said Sarah. She drew her revolver, held it at the ready.

Sven gave Midnight a squeeze, getting closer to Judge Ellison. "Shoot on sight?"

"Normally, no," said the Judge. "Typically, I try to entreat with people, get them to see the error of their ways like I once did. But, this one, what she did to my agent...my friend, I will not grant her a chance at surrender. If we survive, I will perhaps feel remorse."

"And if you don't?" asked Sven.

"Then I will expect God to understand my position."

"And how will we know them? They all wear the same hat or something?"

Sarah laughed, the sound coming from deep within her chest, muffled.

"This mine is supposed to be abandoned, for the gold in its walls went dry before the Slaver's Revolt," said Professor Bass. "If anyone's there, it's them."

The path curved sharply again, back toward the east, all the road ahead hidden by the dense thicket filling the space between the lofty maples.

"Now, we come to the dirty business of it, Silver Pin," said the Judge to Sven. "This is what I have paid for. I will ask you to go first, seeing as you are, as you say, the fastest and most accurate shootist money can—"

Professor Bass, still leading the way, silenced the Judge by swiftly lifting a hand, palm facing the curving path. His five fingers slowly bent so that only his index finger was raised.

All the riders brought their horses to halt and waited.

Sven's heart beat steady and slow. He leveled his keen eye through all the brush, looking for movement. Listening.

They stayed still for a long time, watching the Professor's hand, which never wavered. And then it moved again, forming a circle with thumb and index finger.

At the all clear, Sven quietly dismounted Midnight. Leading him gently by the reins, Sven turned the horse around and hitched him to a sweetgum tree.

He reached into his breast pocket, produced a cigarette and match, and walked past the others to take the vanguard. He stopped for only a moment to strike the match and light the cigarette with a single, long inhalation.

"Our advantage is that we are mounted, Mr. Erickson," said Professor Bass, perplexed. "On foot we lose that—"

"Professor…" Sven took another hard drag from the cigarette, sucking the ember to flare bright and hot. "I am your advantage," he said, his words wreathed in smoke.

"There could be a dozen men up ahead. A mounted rider is provisioned with a tactical—"

"I hear you. But my husband would kill me if something happened to that horse. And speaking of getting killed, you said a dozen men?"

"Ten to twelve is what our agent reported," said the Judge.

"Big number. Professor, how good are you with that pistol?" Sven gestured at the revolver holstered on the man's hip.

"Experienced," said Bass, who then considered further and said with less confidence: "Fairly experienced."

"The Professor is a man of questions," said Sarah, kindly but unvarnished, not of violence."

"May I borrow it, please?" asked Sven.

"Borrow?"

"Yes. I've only got the one." He tilted his head just slightly to gesture at his pistol. "And I'd hate to be caught flat-footed during a reload while I'm at my business of killing these men. Don't you worry though, I will give it back. You have my word."

That got a wide-eyed rise out of Bass: "You plan on taking them all? By yourself."

Sven smiled. "I'm not saying you *can't* come, but, if I have your pistol, I don't like your chances when the smoke begins to fly. No, I figure me and Ms. Lockhart will be plenty of gun." He turned to look over his shoulder at Sarah. "What do you say?"

The afternoon sun struck her teeth as she brandished them like a predator. "After you, handsome."

The Professor handed over his colt dragoon, which had a modified cylinder for cartridge bullets. Sven took it, felt the weight of it in his right hand. It was pearl-handled, shiny as the gates of heaven. "Pretty," said Sven. "And heavy as hell."

"It is accurate," said the Professor.

"If it isn't, it'll certainly work splendidly as a cudgel." He looked to the Judge, who sat with one hand resting on his saddle horn, the other gripping the reins. The big man watched Sven measuring him. Sven knew the look, and it pleased the showman inside of him. He flicked his burning cigarette ahead and said, "We'll be back."

"How will I know if you need help?" asked the Judge. "Will you call out?"

Sven did not turn back. Did not answer.

Sarah followed, then sped up to walk side by side. She drew her pistol from her holster, checking her ammunition. A simple, lightweight single action Army revolver, no frills with the sights filed off.

"You'll want to stay about three paces behind and five or six to the left of me," he said. "If they start shooting and we're too close to—"

"I get it," said Sarah. "This isn't my first rodeo, Silver Pin."

He grinned. "Sorry. Force of habit. You seem the capable shootist."

"How do you figure that? You've never seen me fight. For all you know," she said, jesting, "I could turn yellow the moment the bullets start to fly."

"You?" he asked. "I don't think so. I have an eye for pretenders."

The little road snaked east. All around them, tall grass swayed in a gentle breeze beneath a dense wall of white-flowered shrubs that filled the air with their floral scent. Just ahead beyond that curtain of foliage—no less than a hundred yards, Sven guessed—a motley of voices came. Close enough to hear, too far away to discern their words.

Sven, striding easy and loose up the middle of the road, sank down into the lowest place of his mind. With each step he shed layer after layer of himself. First, his fear fell away. Always first. Fear was the gunfighter's Judas Iscariot, his greatest betrayer. Sinking further, Sven forgot his want to be the One, disabused himself of his joy for the drink and fancy hotel rooms and the life of leisure he so desperately craved. Finally, requiring the greatest effort, he stripped himself of his love for Larry Cornish. Descending deeper and deeper, so that there was no thought, no feeling, he removed all his desire, all his charm, all his hopes and dreams, all that he was until he became only a creature of cold perception. The living embodiment of precision.

Peeling these things away unburdened him, revealed the soul of the man in waking life: Sven Erickson, greatest living gunfighter the world over, perhaps the most dangerous human being to ever step the Earth.

And approaching full of purpose and intent, barely aware of Sarah's footsteps behind him, he spied his target. At the terminus of the dirt- and pebble-strewn path, an open mineshaft gaped wide and dark in high contrast to the bright sunlight streaming from above. At the mouth of the shaft, a lookout leaned against the timber beam composing the entry. The bored-looking man twirled a skinning knife along his fingers, then, quick as a cat, he turned and threw the knife. It sliced through the air, end over end, and pierced the cross-timber, half-blade deep, handle quivering.

Sven continued forward, unseen, toward the lookout.

The man wore a kind of military get-up. Black cloth, buttoned from throat to waist in brass, with a flower-like symbol unknown to Sven embroidered upon the breast in gold. A duo of bandoliers, braced with pistols, made an 'X' across the man's chest. He walked over, plucked the knife from the timber post, and then lazily turned to look down the road. His brow wrinkled. "Hey, Lemmy, we got a couple comin' up this a'way," he said, standing before the open mouth of the mineshaft.

Sven continued forward, squeezing his right hand into a fist, then relaxing. Squeezing with a step, relaxing with the next. Over and over.

"The Baroness and Ike?" asked a voice from the darkness, bewildered.

"Nah, some feller and a Black lady," said the guard. "Hey, stop where you are. Identify yourself!"

"You wasted them, kid," said Sven.

The guard cocked his head. "Wasted what?"

"The last words you'll ever say." And he drew, fired, spun the gun twice, and holstered it again before the guard's body hit the ground.

"Holy shit." Sarah let out a breath.

Sven, denuded of his hopes and loves and enthusiasms, robed only in the blood-red intent of the mercenary competitor, did not look to her. And when he spoke into the mine, he lacquered his words in the cool charm he prided himself in. "My name is Sven Erickson, Silver Pin of the Gunfighters Guild. I am providing a chance for you and the rest of your Society to surrender. My employer seems a decent man; he may allow you to live. But if you fight me, you certainly will not. This is my offer, and I voice it only once."

"Judge said to kill them outright," said Sarah.

Sven lowered his voice. "They aren't going to surrender," he said. "But it will make the Judge feel better that I offered."

Lemmy's voice came from the darkness of the mine. "There was only the two of us," he said, the truth of his words revealed by the fear in his voice. "We had a third man, but we sent him to tell our mistress that what she was looking for wasn't here."

"Well, that's a lie," said Sarah.

"Clearly," said Sven. "You are a bad liar, Lemmy. No one sticks around to guard nothing. I was told you and your friends were hired soldiers, but the fact that you have not tried to fire at me from the advantage of darkness means you are either a coward or an abysmal shot. Hell, you might be both. But you aren't a soldier, are you, Lemmy."

Silence.

"Probably a bad shot, but smarter than his dead friend," said Sarah. "He's retreated into the mine where he can get the drop on us, or wait us out until the others arrive. And from what was reported, she always travels with her full complement of men. We should go and tell the Judge, try to ambush them—"

"Or," said Sven, feeling like a devil with heaven on his mind, "we take what the Baroness is after before she gets here." He grinned and headed for the mineshaft.

Sarah clicked her tongue, disapproving. "That is a bad idea. I've been in this outfit for years, Erickson, and I've seen things I understand and things I'll never comprehend. The rule that has served me best is this: I let the weird people handle the weird shit. That means Professor Bass and Judge Ellison."

"I didn't gauge you to be the cautious type," said Sven, almost at the dark aperture of the mine shaft.

"I am telling you," said Sarah, all her disapproval gone, replaced with warning, "do not go into that mine."

Sven did not begrudge her the trepidation,

nor think less of her because of it. In some way, it was a reminder that there were people in the world who were not armored against peril such as he was. Those who rightly held a greater fear of death. But not him. "I will not be forestalled in my mission by a man such as Lemmy the soldier. Now, come on, Ms. Lockhart," he said, sliding humor into his voice, "let's go find this thing and piss off the Society of Prometheus something fierce."

"No," said Sarah, serious and resolute. "You will not go into that mine."

Sven stopped and turned. Even at this moderate distance, he could see the fear in her eyes, the tight line of her lips pressed together. Behind her, the dense thicket was dark and brooding as the woman herself, even in the sunlight of the high afternoon. The shadow of all surrounding them slashed across her aspect, making her seem somehow even more immovable.

"You're serious," he said. Though he'd never admit it to another living person, the way she was staring at him unnerved him, if only for a moment.

"More than serious." Her hazelnut-colored eyes hardened. "Whatever is inside can only be trusted in the hands of those with the knowl-edge to handle it. You and me, that isn't who we are."

He squared his shoulders and let his eyes lean to slits. "Why, Sarah Lockhart, are you threatening me?"

She swallowed hard. "I've seen your draw. Second fastest I've ever seen. You will certainly kill me, but I'm guessing I can at least wing you."

"You'd rather die than see me enter this place."

"I'd rather see us both live, and for you to listen to reason. If you love your life, if you love your husband, listen to me. I've seen what happens to the minds and wills of those who tamper with forces they cannot understand. If I have to draw against you to save your life, well then, fuck it. I will."

Over the course of his life, there had been one, maybe two, moments when he'd felt the hair-raising icicle of fear run down his spine. It was the "love your husband" that gave him that feeling now, and the "I will" that awoke his soul like a ploughshare awakens the earth, for those were the two words Larry had used after Sven asked him, "Do you think you could love me the rest of your life, Larry?"

I will, Sven thought, hearing the voice of his husband. An answer greater than the question had required, spoken without hesitation. Two words, quicker than a fluttering heartbeat, telling the whole story of who Larry was: the man Sven Erickson had fallen in love with. The man he would love forever.

The darkness of the mine, the possibility of ambush, and the strength of Sarah's determination to stop him from tampering with whatever was inside, none of these things would have stopped him. Only at the mention of losing Larry could Sven be so moved.

Admiring this brave and seemingly unflappable woman, he cocked his head to one side. "Grab the others. I'll wait here."

"And you won't go inside?" Her shoulders still coiled with tension, fingers ready to grip, and she stood rigid at the hips: all the markers of a woman ready to fight and never once educated in the art of the quickdraw.

"You have my word," he said. "We will do it your way."

Sarah turned, ran.

Sven turned, waited.

In that little time alone, looking deep into the black aperture, he thought of Larry, hoping he was alright and that all the luck residing in the world was tilted in his favor. With the invisible arms of his heart extended across the vast distance of the half-a-country between them, and with the outstretched fingers of all his love, he tried to deliver the soothing touch, to heal the dark fear he knew to live inside his husband.

"I'm okay," he said, his quiet words resounding as far as love's echo can reach. "You're okay."

CHAPTER TEN

NATCHEZ-UNDER-THE-HILL, MISSISSIPPI
MARCH 18, 1866

The Silver Pins, led by Michael Horner, disembarked from the Red River King and made their way up the high rocky bluffs, where the avenues of Natchez On-the-Hill shone clean and bright. Finding no leads, the trio descended again to the shadowy, muddy streets of Natchez Under-the-Hill, where they made their way toward the Trumpet Creeper. The trio passed slouched saloons and stone gambling houses where grimy-handed vendors sold rancid fish and crab, and pale meat advertised as choice-cut pork. Streaming along those chopped-up streets, which churned with vice and the steady thrumming rush of the Mississippi, were stumbling drunks and wild-eyed whores, their watchful pimps in high-collared waistcoats never far away. The soiled doves, dressed in tattered corsets, called out from leaning alleyways and tilted doorframes. Through one shadow-bathed doorway of an establishment bearing no sign, Larry was certain that he glimpsed the lower-half of a body as it was dragged out of sight, never to be seen again. A victim of cutthroat thieves.

Horner had seen it too, but when he went to say something, perhaps to protest or to inter-vene, Moody said, "Not our problem, Twelve. Keep on walking."

Larry hated this place. The odors. The discord. Almost every little bit of it.

All but the Trumpet Creeper: four stories tall, painted pink as a peach with trim whiter than a church house, its many glass windows caught the afternoon sun the way a high moon sets ablaze the eyes of a midnight lover. The Creeper was a beauty untouched by the rotting venality spread over the rest of the city.

Inside, they were greeted by a slender Black woman in a yellow silk dress. Her long black hair was braided tight as a rawhide rope. She took the breath from Horner and melted the smile off Moody's smug face. Horner caught his breath again, introduced himself, and announced their purpose.

"Gentlemen," said the woman, bashful in lieu of chiding, "your hats."

Perhaps it had been the lowness of this part of the city, perhaps the beauty of the Creeper or the madam inside, but all three had forgotten the custom. Each removed his hat.

"I'm Lorane Camanule, the chief gardner paramour of the Trumpet Creeper, and I have word for you. Those animals who attacked our brother paramour are a part of a gang known as the Mississippi Junction Boys. They are known well—they frequent the ice house during the heat of the day, make trouble by night. I barred them from this establishment just a month ago for their behavior."

"Terrible," said Horner. "Intolerable."

"How many?" asked Moody, like a man with little time to spare. "In the gang."

"Why, sir," she replied, untouched by his lack of manner, "I couldn't say. I would hate to guess and be wrong."

"Does it matter how many?" asked Horner. "I'm not scared of—"

Moody grit his teeth. "Of course it matters, you cunt-struck idiot. If it's five, maybe ten, then we have no worry. If it's fifty goddamn men, then it's a considerable problem."

"Irrelevant," said Larry, caring little for Horner's hurt feelings and even less for the company of Moody. "Survey at a distance. Spot the three. Take them when in smaller numbers."

"Sharp," said Camanule, batting her eyes at Larry.

Moody saw it and laughed. "Your charms won't work on this one, paramour. He's...got a woman's intimate tastes. And a husband to boot."

"And you are alone, Eight," said Larry, slow and undiminished by Moody's attempt to rile his anger. "Meaning nothing to everyone lacking a silver pin."

Moody didn't miss a beat. "The pin is all that matters to me, Nine."

"Suggest you hold it tight then. One day, you will lose it."

"Maybe." He took a moment to stare hard at Larry. "But not today and never by you."

Larry met the gaze, unwavering. "Perhaps."

"You gonna kill me, Larry Cornish?" asked Moody, more a dare than a question.

"Gentlemen," said Camanule. "You are too dangerous to threaten, so I will beseech you. You clearly have trouble with each other, but you will not bring that trouble into this establishment."

"Listen, whore—" snapped Moody.

"No, Mr. Moody," she said. "You will listen. If beseeching fails, I will command. You are under the employ of Reine Silvia, and I, as an extension of our Queen of the Many Flowered Field's power, demand you to comply or be released from your duty."

"Release me?" He spun on her, eyes flaring. "Release *me*?" Bitch, I do not think you know who you are talking–"

"Moody," said Larry, cautious and careful. "Calm down."

"Don't take that placating tone with me, you goddamn poof," he said, eyes still trained on Camanule.

The woman, unfazed and with hands set atop her stomach, regarded the gunfighters with a kind of distant appraisal, as if she were watching all these things unfold from behind unshatterable glass.

All of Moody's cool had melted in the sundering heat of his vainglory, at the notion that she held any power over him. "I'm the best goddamn chance your whore queen has at—"

Horner, fast as his skills allowed, drew his pistol and pressed it into the gunfighter's cheekbone.

Moody's hands, which had been lifted in fury, were fast, but not fast enough to overtake the draw of a Silver Pin at such close proximity. And Horner had heard enough. He acted on pure instinct, making him as fast as he needed to be in that moment. It was clear he did not care for the mistreatment of women, no matter their station. And for the first time since Sven had come into his life, Larry was genuinely surprised by another man.

"Horner–" said Moody.

"Shut the fuck up," warned Horner, relishing having turned the tables on a gunfighter greater than he would ever be. "You will not speak to this woman in such a fashion. I will not tolerate it."

Moody sneered and pressed his face hard into Horner's pistol, sinking the barrel deeper into his cheek, unafraid. With eyes cold as a winter moon, he stared down the sights of that killing device, boring a hole into its operator. "Don't miss," he said, the words flecked with ice.

Larry took a deep breath, watching the stalemate. In their faces he discerned two things: Michael Horner was an honorable man, if uncouth. Paul Moody was a lunatic. A lunatic with an Achilles heel.

Horner broke away first. "This woman is an extension of our employer," he said, slowly taking his gun away from Moody's cheek. A little round impression remained in his skin, sooty with gunpowder. "And she should be treated as such. With respect."

Moody made no motion to wipe the gunpowder mark from his cheek. "Alright, Twelve," he said, and in his voice was a malevolent want for the highest level of revenge. His eyes slashed over to Camanule. "I'm going to the ice house to find these men, but I can't guarantee they'll be alive when I deliver them to your queen—not with the mood I'm in. You better send her a telegram to prepare her for that disappointment."

Camanule, looking regal and proud, said, "You will refuse to give your patron what she has paid for?"

Moody slowly shook his head, "No matter if she demanded by rights as my patron or begged me now. I am not in the giving vein today." Moody slanted his discontent at Larry and slammed the door of the Trumpet Creeper on his way out.

"Mr. Horner," said Camanule. "Reine Silvia has paid a great deal of gold for the quality of Silver Pin work. My mistress gave her money for three men to be taken alive. If they are produced at her feet in any other fashion, she will be displeased. Word will spread far about her dissatisfaction with your guild work. As far as her fields flower within the country, which is to say, near all of it. Surely, for the sake of your reputation, the two of you can reel in your friend."

"Not likely," said Larry. He knew Moody's reputation and now he had seen the man's mania displayed twice over. Both times Moody had proven his grit, his fearlessness. And shown the killer in his eyes.

"You will do something then," she said, her words sharp all over.

"We will try," said Horner, tipping his hat.

"If you do not bring those men back alive, then I suggest you return back to...wherever it is you Silver Pins come from. I have no use for the flesh of dead men and no time for three incapable gunfighters."

Horner, quick to obey, eagerly tugged Larry by the sleeve. "Come on, maybe we can talk some sense into him."

"No," said Larry, heading out the door and down the steps. "No more talk. Moody is set to kill."

The two gunfighters headed north toward the ice house in lock-step with each other, pressing their way through the crowded streets. The road had been relatively vacant when they arrived, but now it overflowed with gamblers, mendicants, and cutpurses. A stampede of brawny rivermen, some dressed too fancy for their trade and tatterdemalions all the rest, swept up Larry and Horner for a moment, jostling their shoulders and separating them.

"Where is he?" cried Horner, cutting around a tottering drunk holding a wine bottle in each hand.

Larry, peering through the gaps of candlestick-shaped hollows made by the shoulders of hatted men walking side by side, saw no sign of Moody. Somewhere off in the distance near the unseen river, a steamboat bell pealed, and the shrill cry of her whistle cut the air, and Larry felt very lost. Confused. People streamed all around him. More than once he felt the greasy pickpocket touch of thieves, but he could not discern whose hands they were among the swarm of traffic. And so he cinched his hand to the butt of his revolver and opened wide all the power of his keen perception. Scanning the field of transient flesh, he looked for Horner, for no more did he hear the gunslinger calling out.

Across the street, two ragged women tussled with each other, eyes blazing white and wild against the black grime upon their snarling faces. Nearby, a man rubbed his forehead in frustration, likely the cause, object, and subject of the fight. It was the kind of thing Sven would have pointed out, laughed at, but for Larry, shoved by the motley press of travelers toward an alleyway where river fog and malicious darkness roiled, there was panic building, coiling a vice-like grip around his heart. For all he knew, Moody was in that secret black of that alley, drawing his pistol. Aiming slow. Ready to pull the trigger in shadow, so that he might face off against Sven in the hot afternoon light of a future day. The crowd shoved Larry nearer and nearer, and, acting on instinct, he suddenly drew his pistol and aimed the killing end into the vast infinity of the shadow before him.

The gun outstretched, not quite trembling

but nowhere near steady, caught a lance of light. The light made the polished metal of the revolver shine against the swirling emptiness. And Larry, breathing heavy, his face pearled with sweat, cocked the hammer of the revolver and in a harsh whisper asked the darkness a question.

"Moody?"

Fog coiled up the lance of light, thick and gray as woodsmoke and the darkness gave no reply.

A shot rang out, its repeat echoing down the alley where no flash of fire had come. Larry spun. Someone howled, "Christ!"

The clamor of Natchez Under-the-Hill reached a crescendo, a discord of confusion and panic, fear.

"Who shot—"

"Is he dead?"

"Who is he?"

Larry holstered his pistol, turned away from the impotent darkness that had so easily unmanned him and shoved his way roughly through the crowd, no longer afraid. "Horner?" he called out, but so loud and so many were the questions coming from the crowd that his own went unheard and unanswered.

Until Larry sliced through the hurricane cloud of people encircling the placid eye where the body lay.

There, crumpled in a fetal position, eyes flat

and with a grievous wound set between them, lay Michael Horner.

Larry kneeled. Examined. Pitied this man who, though he might never have become who he hoped to be, deserved better than to be ambushed by the likes of Paul Moody.

"I'm real sorry, mister," came a masculine voice from behind Larry. "Was he your friend?"

The gunfighter reached over, picked up the hat Horner had been wearing. He placed it atop the man, hiding the vacant death mask of the twelfth fastest quickdraw the world over. "No," replied Larry. "Colleague."

"Well, I suggest you handle your man's body right away, or the rats will come and strip him of all he has. Leave him naked in the street. Then the other rats will come and take what remains."

Larry nodded and, wanting no indignity to befall a rival and gunfighter who had loved the game, he paid two men twenty dollars each to help him carry the body back toward the Trumpet Creeper.

They set Horner upon the steps, and Larry asked the men to wait a moment. Then, he went inside and, with a cold demeanor and uncompromising voice, addressed Camanule.

"Dead," said the woman, the embodiment of calm. "That is a shame; he seemed well-meaning."

"As an extension of your patron's power, so

too are you an extension of her responsibility," said Larry. "You will see the body sent to the House of the Gun, New Orleans. His remains unsullied and his property whole."

She accepted without a moment's hesitation. "Yes. You will still see to your mission, as I will see to this?"

"If Moody has not already extended his killing to those your patron seeks? Yes."

Camanule's face wrinkled for the first time, trying to comprehend. "This goes against the rules of your guild, correct? I thought your people only fought one another in duels."

"Yes," said Larry, his voice sounding cold and thin in his own ears. "When I find Paul Moody, it will be the last duel of his life."

He pushed his way out of the Trumpet Creeper, told the two men still standing sentinel over the body to wait for instructions, and then, to ensure the request would be followed, promised them another fifty dollars each. And he looked over the body of Michael Horner. The young man might never have held in his hands the ability to attain the rank of One, but he'd still been a guild member, worthy of challenge.

Larry drew in his breath, let it out slow, feeling within himself the dark, imperishable rage swell and intensify with every heartbeat. In this way, the paramour St. Guy had been a protected member of Reine Silvia's conjugal retinue, a flower beaten into the earth because men had decided that such a beauty could not exist in their ugly world. The Mississippi Junction Boys. Paul Moody. Different in their aspect, all too similar in the way they interacted with the world around them, men who believed that the world must shift on the wind of their moods.

Larry removed the silver pin from where it was pinned to his vest and set it brazenly upon the breast of his coat so that all could see. So that all would know: to engage with this man was, at best, to risk peril; at worst, to court destruction. Then his feet were moving, headed north. Every shadow-filled alley he passed, he gazed into, no longer panicked at what they held but examining each with a malevolent hope he would spy Paul Moody waiting. He shoved through the press of people, saying nothing while meeting with killing countenance any tilted, prying eye looking to interlope in his affairs.

The heat of the sun overhead and teeming mass of bodies all around him only stoked his hot, inconsolable rage. North he went, scanning the streets with predator perception until at last he came to a rude, brown structure bearing in faded white paint the words 'Hill Ice.' Next to its simple door, a freckle-faced woman with fire-red hair leaned against the wall. She was strapped with a pistol, smoking a cigarette.

Hearing his footfalls approach, she met his

eyes and smiled with the confidence granted to practitioners of violence who have known the chimes of battle and lived to recount their music. She opened her mouth to speak but stopped short when her eyes flicked to his right. Her confidence melted like wax at the descent of the candle flame. "Shit," was all she said.

"Guild business," said Larry. "Three men, friends of yours, assaulted a paramour. I've come to collect them."

"You can't just—"

"Few can," he said. "I am one of them. You have two minutes to deliver these men, unarmed, to me. If they are not here, you will give me their precise location. Go inside. Tell your boss, your people, what you see. Inform them. My name is Larry Cornish of the Silver Pin rank. If you require me to force my way in, you will be the first among many to die." Then he flicked his chin at her. "Time starts now."

"I...I don't—"

Stealing a trick from Sven, he slowly drew his pistol from his holster and, examining the killing device, began to slowly cycle the cylinder. Each click resounded like the ticking of a clock. He flicked his eyes up to meet hers. "Every second is precious."

Staring at Larry, perhaps afraid he would shoot her if she turned away, she opened the door of the ice house, backed inside, then closed it.

There came from within those walls the sound of screaming and yelling, a symphony of panic. Larry stepped two paces back, squared his shoulders, and holstered his revolver.

The clock of his mind counted slowly. Twenty-five. Forty. Sixty. His heart, though never hurried, began to sink at the prospect of having to fulfill the promise of his threat.

He took a deep breath, saying to himself, "Ninety."

From beyond the door came more screaming, more loud protests, and the discord that comes from the human throat at the knowledge of betrayal. And, coming close to the terminus of his measurement of time, he pivoted from counting up to counting down.

"Fifteen," he said, then inhaled. "Ten." The exhalation whistled through gritted teeth.

"…out there, goddamn you, Pete! You'll kill us all!"

"Five," said Larry, closing down his senses to center his focus on the work now only three seconds away. He took a step forward.

The door broke open and a tumbled mass of three men were forcibly shoved out into the street. They landed splayed out in the mud. Two remained there, stunned by the hard impact. The third, a blond man whose ratty clothes were now caked in wet mud, scrambled to his feet and rushed to re-enter the ice house like a sinner crying sanctuary before an unwelcoming tabernacle. The door slammed shut, and he pounded on the heavy door, his fists falling with desperate thudding impacts. "Boss!" he howled. "Boss, don't do this!"

"Take 'em," came the voice of a man within the ice house.

The two lying in the street turned their gazes upon Larry in unison, and the blood drained from their mud-streaked faces.

"Boss!" the blond man screamed, his voice cracking. "Please, lemme in! You're fucking us. You are fucking us!"

"No," said Larry.

At the sound of his voice, the man turned, mouth opened wide in silence. Their eyes met.

"You fucked yourself."

CHAPTER ELEVEN

THE CONSOLIDATED SILVER FIELD MINE, NEAR CHARLOTTE, NORTH CAROLINA MARCH 18, 1866

"It's was a good plan," said Professor Bass, his stormy eyes and smirking face illuminated by an oil lamp in the darkness of the mine. "If perhaps a bit overconfident."

The Judge wiped sweat from his brow with a coat sleeve. "Well, I expected a simple mine shaft, not a fucking maze, Robert." And he looked to Sven, who was sitting on a crate, one leg crossed over the other. "We've missed something."

The gunfighter guessed that they had missed quite a bit. The mine was all shot through with dark, humid tunnels branching off from the main shaft, and they had traced many of them. Some had come to dead ends, others wound back toward the main shaft in infuriating circuits. "Time runs thin before this Baroness shows up with all the men you hired me to kill."

The Judge, looking every second of his near sixty years of age, rubbed his nose and spat. "Think," he said to himself. "*Think.*"

"We could split up," said Sven. "Cover more ground more quickly."

Both the Professor and the Judge gave him pitying glances. "No," they said in unison, the echo of their loud voices tiptoeing down the tunnel and then back up to reverberate their protest.

"No what?" Sarah called out from her position as lookout at the open mouth of the shaft.

"Don't worry about it," the Judge called back. "Any sign?"

"Nothing!"

A gale, sudden and cold, rushed from the darkness, sending pebbles and dust up the length of the main shaft. On the wings of that wind billowed a word, whisper-sharp: "Nothing."

Sven, as brave and bold as any man to cross the plain of the world, felt his blood run cold.

"Nothing..." the word came again. Longer this time, the vowel drawn out like the breath of a dying man.

Sven slid off the crate. "The fuck is—"

"Shh," hissed Professor Bass, and so quickly did the temperature drop that a jet of steam clouded about the lantern clutched in his upraised hand.

"Careful." The Judge's voice was low and commanding.

"Careful of what?" Sven reached for his revolver, found the wooden grip cold as a block of ice.

The Judge swallowed hard. "I don't know."

And from the shuddering cold and blackness, the voice did not speak but pronounced a dissonate sound wide and deep. Musical. The note deepened and intensified, reverberated along the once wet stone walls now whited with hoarfrost. Sven stepped to the center of the shaft, gun in hand, and slowly walked toward the sound, listening.

The voice continued, needless of breath, and the long note dipped again, below the possibility of human range. It grew in intensity as it sank into the ocean of its sound, fathoms deep, and deeper still, drawing him closer. And Sven found himself walking further down the main shaft. The wind came again. Colder. So cold that he felt the pearls of his chilled sweat harden to freeze upon his face. But it was of no matter. Nor did he care for the voices battling the song, crying out his name, begging. A finger of wind slid across his wrist, and at the invisible command of its touch, he let the gun fall from his fingers. One foot in front of the other, he stepped into an ever-widening night that beckoned. Had beckoned in a time before there were nations and cities to claim. Before men and life and the world. Before light and darkness were separated, this song had reigned. And from the void, a hand unseen placed itself upon Sven's frost-dimpled cheek. Caressing, gliding across his flesh.

It was the touch of a lover, a father, a sibling returned for a long, long journey—the full measure of longing finally fulfilled.

Tears filled his eyes, freezing so quickly that a single wet blink sealed his eyelids shut. He had no need of his sight now, though. For the song filled his shuttered eyes with vision. It cupped the hand of its sound to his ear and whispered every truth vested within the annals of the universe. And then lips emanating the song settled soft and wet upon his mouth and flooded him with music. He felt the wind of time, the cold of space, and truth itself fill him. The song was all, and this unseen singer the deliverer.

All hopes happily dashed. All joys shattered. All love irrelevant.

All prospect a sham, and life a losing game.

Ecstasy. Bliss. Rapture.

These things took him and the world around him.

We Do Not
Say the Name

ABOARD THE STEAM TRAIN
HEPHAESTUS
CHARLESTON, SOUTH CAROLINA

Dear Claramay,

I am more than victorious. How proud of me you will be, how elated, when I tell you I was wrong. In the fever of my zeal for this great cause, I made a mistake, my love. You, my truest and deepest love, who I abandoned when I should have gathered. I gave myself over to doubt and selfishness, but I should have trusted you, Glory. Should have told you everything as our hands were laced together, vows made, and said, "Come with me."

Forgive me this, Claramay. Forgive it all.

I thought I understood the measure of the world I would be forced to live in and the requirements of my great teacher. The High Priest has written me though, and in his letter was the salve to all our pain and loss. The repair to my dereliction of you. A letter filled with a wisdom too deep for my young mind to comprehend. I was sure, so sure, my love, that this life demanded isolation and a singular focus to a grand purpose. But I have won a great victory, and now I am afforded my Roman Triumph.

There is much to tell you, and all of it I wish could be heard rather than read in a letter. And I wonder, Claramay, in the long month that has passed since my mistake of leaving you, can you still hear my voice in every written word? Do you still in your mind walk in the secret garden of our hearts? If so, I hope you will search among our many flowers and find forgiveness blossoming there. Ours were many years of sunshine, which made that garden grow. And for a month, the rains of sadness have flooded our precious place. Hear me, my heart, when I say that clouds can break to show once again the smiling face of the sun. And in this letter I can say what I should have said on our wedding day. Trusting you to see what I see: a world set right.

My enemies plotted against me in North Carolina. Malicious and delusional, vicious in their ways, they killed my trusted friends and plotted to take from me that which does not belong to them. They laid in wait, Clara. Desiring to first steal the object of my mission and then destroy the life of the woman you fell in love with. They set themselves against a purpose they cannot understand. Against order and against the reformation of a world aching to remember all as it once was. They are my enemies, my love. And soon, they will be your enemies, too. They are known as the Peregrine Estate. Their chief actor a traitor to the cause. His name is Judge Hezekiah Ellison, the falconer whose many dangerous birds he has hired specifically to maim and destroy those who believe in true equality—our sacred purpose. His agents, all of them specialists of elite skill, reach far and wide in America, perhaps in Europe and Asia too. The man's intimate knowledge of our ways makes him the greatest adversary—our society's Benedict Arnold. And further still, in addition to aiming his estate's full strength against us, he has spent a portion of his incalculable wealth to hire a member of the Gunfighters Guild. For so fearful he is, and so filled with an irrepressible wrath, that he brought to bear a Silver Pin. And had not the hand of determinate fate intervened, his plans would have succeeded.

But it did, my glory. It did.

The object I was sent to procure, a sphere of ancient stone with properties I will never totally ken but have greatly studied, was procured by one of my men. Its strange power coursed through him. But then the stone, in an act of self-preservation, throbbed to life. Refusing to fall into the hands of the Judge, it crushed the mind of the Silver Pin. The Judge's agents, completely unmoored by the stone's tactic, tried to destroy my man and the stone. But the

Silver Pin, his mind taken over, no longer fought for the Judge's purpose but for my own.

The Judge and his birds were scattered upon my approach, retreating as the cowards they are, rather than die as I would have—a martyr.

Throwing my enemies to the wind, Claramay, I fearlessly approached the Silver Pin and commanded him. He listened. Obeyed.

My men demanded that I take his life, but they do not have the vision I do. The long sight to be able to see a hazard transformed into an asset. Aboard the Hephaestus, *the mighty steam train gifted to me by the High Priest, I have come to Charleston with prisoner and power in tow. Having attained the stone, disarmed my enemies of their mercenary weapon, and gained the illimitable favor of our Society's author and architect, my life and purpose are almost full. There is only one thing now missing:*

You.

Claramay, in my deep desire to achieve that which must be done for the correction of a world set upon incorrect course, I navigated away from that which makes the world worth saving. My hands, even when full, feel empty without the touch of your skin. My mouth aches to remember your sweetness. Yearns to once again have you set yourself as a chalice before my lips, that I might drink and drink and drink until we are both satisfied. All the world is absent of your scent. And where I only a month ago believed that in fulfilling the Society's purpose I would know completion, I now realize there can never be completion without you.

Come to me, Claramay. Come to Charleston. Let us walk barefooted upon the sand and gaze unto the impossibly wide blue of the Atlantic until the bowl of the sun is poured out, turning the waters to gold.

Forgive me all my many faults and the pains I have caused. Allow me to fulfill my promise, make my vows, and marry you.

You.

Always and forever you, Clara.

And I, always and forever yours,

Gwenny

CHAPTER TWELVE

HOUSE OF THE GUN
NEW ORLEANS, LOUISIANA
MARCH 29, 1866

Down the Mississippi Larry Cornish had come after depositing the trio of Junction Boys into the hands of Lady Camanule. The return to New Orleans went slow. The river, though widened and deepened by the spring floods, was overstuffed with wharf boats and steamers too many to count. He spent the hours and days in quiet reflection, sequestered to either his cabin or a lonely table in the steamboat's grand saloon. His mind, like the river, was flooded with regret for the loss of Michael Horner, hatred for Paul Moody, and worry for what would come next. Where had Moody gone, and would he be lying in wait? Would the Gold Pins believe Larry's tale of what happened? When would he see Sven again?

It was this last question that plagued him the most between the blaze of dawn and the shadow of his restless nights when he found no longer found solace in the scent of his husband's tobacco. The questions preyed on him so heavily that the beauty of the river gave no peace, whiskey no dulling effect, and the saloon food bore no taste. Even when leaning upon the railing of the hurricane deck, where he gazed upon a spray of blue and red and purple wildflowers lining the riverbank, he searched for his simple delight in their color but was left only wanting. These moods were known to him, and not uncommon before Sven had come into his life. Sven's companionship had driven away the predatory melancholy and overwhelming loneliness. And now, separated for this small measure of time from the man he loved, the internal sorrow he'd carried his whole life returned, exhausting him though he made no labor.

The midnight hour on the third day of his journey saw gaslighted New Orleans pour over the horizon. The city was crowned in smoke billowing from foundry stacks, the streets teemed with foot traffic, and the sound of fifes and drums and fiddles slid across the cobblestone streets to skip upon the face of the Mississippi.

Larry disembarked and walked along the wharf, where a man and woman, both of them wide-eyed romantics, clasped hands as only lovers may do, astonished with the dark beauty of unsleeping New Orleans. The man turned the woman at the shoulders, cupped her at the small of her back, and lay into her a long, deep kiss. And the woman, reaching with fingertips to touch the smooth skin of his young, cool face, gave herself over to the power of the moment. The making of a memory. Their dream come to life.

Larry looked away, almost ashamed of himself, unable to enjoy the happiness of others.

He paid a buggyman twenty cents and was ushered through the night toward the House of the Gun. Over the clumped clip-clops of the buggy horse's traversal upon the cobblestone streets of New Orleans, Larry honed the edge of his memory to quickly and accurately recall to the Gold Pins the events in Natchez Under-the-Hill. There was much to report and, more importantly, the possibility of some waiting message or word of Sven's progress either in his mission or of that of his return.

After passing through near the whole of the city, and once again displaying the implements and ornaments of his association to the gate attendant, Larry Cornish walked up the pebbled path which led to the House of the Gun. Boris, clad in a brass-buttoned navy suit, greeted Larry warmly at the door. "Well met, Nine," said the attendant, with more uncertainty than usual in that otherwise professional tone of his. The collective of his crow's feet creased, forming a concerned squint. "Your companions?"

"A conversation for the Gold Pins," said Larry.

"Ms. Starr is settled in the drawing room, meeting with a potential proxy." said Boris, dipping his head and stepping back so that the door opened wide. "The other Gold Pins are dispatched on errand. Shall I request an audience, or prepare a room for you, that you might speak with her in the morning?"

"Tonight," said Larry, entering the hallowed hall where the portraits of Gold Pins wavered in the candlelight.

"Yes, sir. If you would so kindly." Boris extended his hand.

Larry gave over his gun and waited.

Boris stepped along the checkered marble floor, never rushed, shoulders erect. Behind his desk was the pistol station, a series of honeycomb-colored cubbies cut from one piece of wood. The old man ran a hand along the wooden edge, finding the appropriate slot where he set the revolver. Five-by-five, every square bore a little silver plaque, each of them numbered, all of them empty now save the nine slot where Larry's gun lay.

A few moments later, a slender Black man

turned out of the drawing room. As he passed by, he met Larry's gaze, but only a nod passed between them. The man exited the House of the Gun, and another minute passed before Boris stepped into the hall. "Ms. Starr will see you now, Nine."

Larry removed his hat and headed down the hall, listening to the singular echoes of his footfalls, which he desperately longed to be two pairs.

In the drawing room, he found Belle Starr standing before the great, roaring hearth, gowned in layered ruffles of periwinkle silk with white sheer accents. Her long curls were drawn back in a heavy bun, head crowned with a crescent of foxfire marigolds twisted through snowy jasmine vine. She smiled and greeted him. "Hello, Nine."

"Ms. Starr," said Larry.

"I find it troubling to see one Silver Pin approach where I had expected a visit from three."

"The Eight broke the rules of our association and shot the Twelve in the street without entering into contest. Michael Horner is dead."

She said nothing, a portrait of composure. "I'll hear the whole of it. Won't you sit?" She moved to one of the wingback chairs before the fire. When she sat down, she found Larry standing before her, hat in his hands.

"I will stand," he said.

"If it pleases you, though I'm sure you are tired from your trip and this alleged betrayal."

Wasting no time, Larry recounted the events of Horner's death simply and in their order.

"And that is the whole of it?" she asked.

"Of that piece, yes," said Larry. "I captured the assailants. All three alive, as contracted."

Belle Starr looked away, considering, then watched her own hand drum softly on the chair's leather arm. "I know you are spartan in your speech pattern, Nine, but I feel an eagerness in you to be done with this conversation, that we might have another. A discussion regarding word of your husband."

"There is word?" said Larry, uncharacteristically rushed.

"Yes. Though I worry in telling you this news that you would make a rash decision."

Larry's heart, like a stone cast from the father of all earthly cliffs, fell.

Belle's eyes, shaped by worry, colored in firelight, flicked to meet his gaze. "Per Judge Ellison's most recent telegram, your husband engaged his patron's enemies and was taken captive. Ellison's agents attempted to help him, but strangely—most strangely, Larry—your husband opened fire on them. The agents were forced to flee, barely surviving your husband and barely eluding capture by those whom they originally pursued."

The stone of Larry's heart, falling and falling and falling, collided into an ocean of fear, sinking fathoms deep. "Why—" The word near soundless.

"The Judge did not say, nor is it my place to ask. A patron's coin affords them a Silver Pin and all the Guild's discretion. However, stranger still is this: the Judge informs us that he is headed to Charleston, where he will attempt to reclaim your husband. He says Sven is not to blame for acting a traitor. And there it is. I see, Larry Cornish. At this very moment, in your eyes, I see action building. You know that in paying for one Silver Pin, unable to afford another, the Guild's rules will not allow you to intervene."

"Rules," said Larry.

"Nine, as an artisan of the Guild and member of our association, robed in the protections and enterprise it affords you as a gunfighter, I beg you to keep our rules. Honor the vows you have made to the House of the Gun, which sheltered and shielded you during your rise in rank. As a Silver Pin, you are required to remain here. As a Gold Pin, I am entrusted to ensure that you do."

"You would kill me."

"With regret," said Belle Starr. "And right where you stand."

"Even though I am unarmed."

"We both know that wouldn't change the outcome."

Feeling his stone heart come to rest at the bottom of the ocean inside him, Larry took a deep breath. Let it out. Relaxed.

"Larry," said Belle, compassion sweetening her tone, "The Judge and his agents are going after your husband. It might be they succeed. Don't waste your last breath attempting to—"

"I retire," said Larry.

Belle's eyes flared, her brow crinkled below the marigold and jasmine crown. And for a moment, the only sound within the drawing room was the crackling cylinders of wood within the fire. Then, the Gold Pin asked, "Retire?"

"From the game, the players, and all vows made to this, your House of the Gun."

"By retiring you make yourself a mark for the reputation-building of others. You remove all protections the Silver Pin affords. Any may challenge, pin or no, and this includes the enemy you have made of Paul Moody by naming him a vow-breaker."

"I have no fear of future challenge or challenger."

"No," she said, appraising him with empathy and understanding. "You fear only life without him."

"I do," he said.

"And what if he is already dead, Larry?" she

asked softly. "What will you do if you get up to Charleston and find that he was gone even before you made this choice?"

He gave the Gold Pin the fullness of his honesty. "Destroy his killers. To the very last man."

"I will accept your retirement, Nine, on one condition. Should you succeed in this rescue and return to your arms the man you love, you will also return to me my Eleven."

What years ago would have seemed an impossibility in the face of his desire to command the respect of the world, Larry Cornish accomplished with ease. He reached up and pulled free of his breast the needled icon. And, in removing the silver number, in choosing to be more than just a competitor in the country's most harrowing game, Larry changed. He felt it. Felt the weight of the game fall away. Felt his melancholy turn to ash within the fires of his heart. And where he had for many years allowed the pin to define him to all the world, for this moment on, it would be his love for Sven Erickson that would be the mark of his identity.

Belle Starr stood up, the blue of her dress catching the wavering firelight, and she held out her hand, a sad smile perched on her lips.

Larry gave over the Nine pin, sliding it into her open palm.

"Equal luck," she said. "To each of you."

CHAPTER THIRTEEN

SOLOMON HALL
CHARLESTON, SOUTH CAROLINA
MARCH 31, 1866

"Is he broken?" The question came from a far off place. The voice young. Female.

"Broken?" Another woman. "How do you mean?"

"I mean, outside of being limited by his gender, doctor. Is he to recover?"

Consciousness had returned to Sven Erickson, then his hearing, and now the sensation of touch. Two hands, small and delicate, lightly pressed along his throat to feel his pulse. He kept his eyes closed and made no motion. He was on his back, head propped up on a soft pillow. The humid air did nothing to cool the pearls of sweat he felt beaded along the entirety of all his naked flesh. His ankles and wrists constricted by knotted ropes chaffed raw his wrists and ankles.

A pressure fell upon the mattress, someone sitting near him now. The breath of a sigh touched his damp brow. "Hmm, his pulse is stronger than before, which is more than we can say for poor Lemmy."

"Yes, poor Lemmy. Ashes to ashes and all that," said the other woman, dismissive.

"Do you want the good news or the bad, Baroness?"

"I'll have them both, Doctor Van Horn."

"Any preference to the order?"

"Doctor. On with it please."

"The bad news is that this patient gives the impression of being comatose."

"I've heard worse."

"The good news is that it is a very bad impression."

"How do you mea—"

"I mean," said the doctor, "he's playing possum."

"Can you blame me?" Sven opened his eyes. Into view, blurry at first, then clearing, came the smiling face of a blonde woman. She wore a smooth buckskin outfit with riding gloves tucked into her waistband. The room behind the doctor's smiling face was all shot through with late morning or early evening light, he did not know which.

"Open your mouth," she said.

Sven pushed his head deeper into the pillow.

The doctor, like a girl fussing with an older brother, said, "You don't want to refuse, sir. If you don't open for me, you will do so at the insistence of my tools. Now," she said and clicked her tongue. "Let's have a look-see."

"Or don't," came the voice of the other woman. The Baroness, lithe as a viper, stepped into view from behind Doctor Van Horn. She peered at Sven, her almond-brown eyes set above cheekbones that would be the envy of any blue-blood aristocrat, and then gracefully tossed her long brown hair behind an alabaster shoulder. "More fun that way."

Sven glared at her.

"Who are you?" she asked, folding her arms across her chest. Her eyes, wide with something close to mania, glittered with sunlight.

"A moment," said the doctor, and she leaned close. Examining. Probing his teeth, gums, and tongue. "Incredible," she said, sliding her fingers from his mouth. "I find you entirely unharmed, save for any lingering effects of your coma. I must say, sir, your fortune and luck were very good as they pertain to your interaction with the stone. Much greater than the man who held it while it was activated."

"Enough, Clara," snapped the Baroness. "Who are you, Silver Pin?"

"A naked man, roped to a bed, wondering how the fuck I got here," he said.

"So, amnesia, too," said the doctor. "Remark-able! The stone not only compelled you to act against your interests, it also wiped your memory of it. Absolutely fascinating."

"That will be all, doctor," said the Baroness, commanding.

"I will go," she said, a smile brightening her face, "so long as you do not harm this subject. Not until I've had ample time to test his resistances to the stone's decaying effect on its host."

"I make no promises," the Baroness replied. "Out."

Van Horn lifted her eyebrows and sighed. She got up from the bed and headed for the door.

"How did you know I was pretending?" asked Sven. "How did you ken that I was awake when I gave no sign."

The doctor paused, trailing a palm down the length of the door frame, and looked back at him. "Your pulse, of course. For whatever a man tries to hide, Mr. Erickson, the heart always gives it away." And then she was gone.

The Baroness drew a chair away from a window, sat down, and crossed her legs. "You may be asking yourself the question, 'How deep in the shit am I right now?', and that's only natural for a man splayed naked and bound in an unfamiliar room. Wonders which way things are about to go for him. Well, let me tell you that you are only in as much shit as you decide to be. I am the Baroness of the Eastern Seaboard, named by a power greater than you or I, and you reside now in that power's familial home as a prisoner. My prisoner. My nature is to be cruel to men with the self-same cruelty they taught to me when I was younger, but I need not be mean, Silver Pin. Answer my questions, give me what I want, and I will offer you more than the Judge ever could. Now, again I will ask, who are you?"

The woman, though young, spoke with a confidence beyond her years. Sven was well practiced at discerning between boldness and bluff, and this woman was not bluffing. "My name is Sven Erickson. I am the Twelve of the Silver Pin rank."

"Twelve of twenty-five, yes?"

"Yes."

"So, of the fastest gunfighters in the world… you're middle of the pack." The Baroness smirked, needling.

"No," said Sven. "I am the fastest."

"That's not what the number suggests."

"Circumstances slowed my rise in rank."

"Has the Judge hired others like you?"

It was Sven's turn to smirk.

The Baroness rolled her eyes, brandished her teeth in a smile. "Other pins. Mercenaries, I mean."

"No," he said.

"Because you were supposed to be enough to handle me and my men."

"He could not afford more, and because I am all he needed."

"You believe that now, even as you are here, made a prisoner."

Sven's pride chaffed at the comment. "How did I get here?"

"Overwhelmed by the power of the stone, forced to act against the interests of those who hired you, by ways even I do not understand. But, one who can understand is on his way."

"Who?" asked Sven.

"We do not say the name."

"I'm surprised you didn't kill me. If I manage to get loose, you will certainly wish you had."

The Baroness giggled, swaying a little, as if charmed by his genuine threat. "Your interaction with the stone makes you an oddity. Doctor Van Horn will compare you against all that remains of Lemmy. She'll look you through and through—flesh, muscle, bone, right down to the soul, which she attests she has means of weighing. And if you prove special, then it will be for the one who sent me to decide your fate."

"So I'm just supposed to wait here," said Sven. "Tied like a Christmas goose."

She placed the flat of her palm upon his chest and slowly slid her fingers down his breastbone, then his stomach. "There are ways to pass the time."

"If your mind is about seduction, I'm afraid you're going to be sorely disappointed at my lack of enthusiasm. My husband owns my heart and the object of your gaze."

Her hand continued its downward glide, sliding over his manhood. "As you are for the male, I am for the female, Mr. Erickson. And this is not seduction," she said, grabbing hold of his testicles and making her hand a vice. The world went white, then black. Sven tried to twist, but the ropes held him fast. Sickness filled his belly, and his heart raced at the crushing pain.

"Fastest gunfighter alive," she said, pure elation in her alto voice, "made like all other men. Brought to heel with ease."

Sven opened his mouth, ready to scream, but she squeezed harder, stealing his breath and sound.

"No," she said. "Shh. Shh. Shh. We don't need anyone hearing our business."

The fire of pain burned up through his pelvis, his stomach, his spine.

"Quiet now, tiger," she said.

Whimpering, he complied, all his capability laid low.

She let a low hum of satisfaction purr from her lips. "Good boy," she said, still squeezing to break, but not destroy. "I am going to count, and when I reach three, I am going to hurt you worse. If your reaction is heard beyond this bed, you will live to regret it."

Sven breathed in and out, sucking a whistle of wind between his gritted teeth.

The Baroness leaned close to his ear, where she ran a finger along his bulging cheek. "Shall we count together?"

CHAPTER FOURTEEN

ABOARD THE STEAM TRAIN
CARDINAL SONG EXPRESS
9:15 A.M.
APRIL 1, 1866

For five days and four nights upon the *Cardinal Song Express*, Larry Cornish had not said a word. Eating little, sleeping less, he was wholly possessed by the churning anxiety known only to those who have faced the potential destruction of a life made whole. Morning came and went, changing the light within his passenger car. Night followed. The moon rose to set its face upon the sky, then sank before him. Exhaustion took hold, but there was little sleep to be found in the shadow of his dreams. The terror of what had happened or might be happening to his husband swirled together with his dark rage, spiraling off into prophetic visions of himself as an annihilating maelstrom, enacting terrible calamity upon the faceless assailants who had dared to harm Sven.Outside the window, America rolled by in grand springtime hues, but he no longer saw the country's portrait beauty. He brooded, considering how to find the Judge via the telegrapher's office and resigning himself to killing him, should the man prove a traitor to Sven's contract. Why else would Sven switch sides and fire upon the Judge's agents?

The more he thought on it, the more it made sense. Ellison had falsified his intent, and Sven had been required to defend himself against that lie.

But if that were the case, why had Sven not sent word to him or to the Guild? He did not know, but he would get answers. Whether by way of coercion, bribery, or force, he would have them.

Deep into the dawn-soaked city of Charleston, the roots of the wide Atlantic Ocean coiled, four winding dark rivers named Wando and Cooper, Stano, and Ashley. The telegrapher's office had been addressed as just east of the Washington Race Course. After having Heartbeat unloaded from the stable car, Larry rode to the racetrack and made his way past the white, Italianate grandstands, overstuffed with hundreds of gamblers in the lather of their habit, watching quarter horses charge and flag, winning for some and costing others all.

He found the telegraph office, designated by a makeshift sign, but the telegraph man was not present, so he waited outside. It was little more than a canvas tent set outside a busy saloon, where sailors, shrimpers, and other hardy boatmen all drank away headaches and ate a free breakfast of cornbread, salt pork, and molasses pinto beans.

When the telegraph man finally arrived, he slowly set up shop and laid open a brass-braced, walnut chest, which held the miraculous device invisibly connecting the country. The gunfighter produced the telegram originally sent to the House of the Gun, brandished the pin upon his chest, and asked for the Judge's location.

"He over at Le Pont d'Ghengis," said the telegrapher, a free Black man prideful enough to be bold in his answer, wise enough not to test Larry's patience. "Big hotel. Can't miss it.' He pointed down one of the cobblestone streets. "Room 902, but he never in there. Got two there with him: a drunk and a pretty lady. Find 'em all in 1204, the pretty lady's room."

Larry tossed him a five-dollar gold piece and rode along the sun-drenched cobblestones, through a crowd of early risen workers and stumbling, bleary-eyed drunks, and past dirty-faced reprobates strewn throughout alleyways. On his right, the Stono River charged, chopped to white in its rush and muddy brown where the waters calmed in their swirl, the whole body swollen by the spring flood season. Just along the waterway, he came to find a portion of the city so recently built that the scent of fresh-cut timber overtook the briny wind blowing in from the Atlantic. Carpenter wagons, their slated contents tarped over, lined the street. Painters were already about their work, whitewashing the little fences and hitching rails and a soaring trellis not yet ready for ivy. Around a bend, set on a corner lot, was a five-story behemoth bearing a fancy sign: Le Pont d'Ghengis. A line of patrons streamed out the door long enough to catch the eye, too thin to be a mob.

Larry hitched Heartbeat nearby, cut through the slender line of those awaiting their chance at breakfast, and walked into the hotel, willing to ask for answers yet ready to kill.

The attendant at the wide, lavish hotel desk greeted Larry almost immediately. "Welcome, good sir." He was thin and chinless, lacking near all masculine features. "If you are here for our shrimp and grits, the line begins outside."

"I am not," said Larry, finding the stairs with his eyes.

"Oh," said the man, perking up. "If you are looking for a room, it is three dollars a—"

"Judge Hezekiah Ellison."

"Ah," he said, and then a curious look came over his face, as if he were waiting for Larry to say something. Then, he said, "Are you with the Judge?"

The phrase was strange.

"No," said Larry.

"And your purpose?" He was still smiling as one hand slipped beneath the desk and out of sight.

"To talk."

"I am happy to send a note up to him, should you be willing to wait."

"You will have to take your hand off that gun in order to pen it," said Larry.

"That is correct," said the attendant. "Shall I do so?"

"If you value your life."

"I do."

"Send your note. Write: Larry Cornish is here, regarding Sven Erickson."

The attendant nodded. "On your honor, sir," he said, then brought his hand back into view. He dipped a pen, put it to paper, and whistled as he scratched the note.

From the kitchen just behind Larry came a scrawny boy wearing a grease-slathered smock. He approached the desk, eager, hands cupped over his chest. "Yes, Mr. Priest?"

"Tommy, this note is for Judge Ellison." The attendant spoke to the boy but kept his eyes trained on Larry. "Check the Judge's room first. If he does not answer, send it to Ms. Lockhart, if you please."

Tommy looked at unblinking Mr. Priest, then to Larry, and back to Mr. Priest. "Umm," he said, all his eagerness melted to nerves.

"It's alright, Tommy. This is Larry Cornish. An honorable man. Now, hurry."

Tommy took the note and rushed up the scarlet-carpeted stairs and around their curved balustrade. Even once out of sight, his footfalls could be heard pounding for two stories and higher, until their sound muffled to nothing.

Larry stared at Mr. Priest.

Mr. Priest stared back, hands resting on the desktop.

Then there came a great noise, the slam of a door followed by heavy, labored footfalls, louder than three Tommy's put together could never hope to make.

"Mr. Cornish," came a booming voice. "Mr. Cornish." Around the bend of the stairs came the big man Larry had seen making his case in the House of the Gun, but this time Judge Ellison was in a near state of undress. The braces of his black trousers were looped at the waist and stretched around the shoulders of a long shirt stained at the armpits, and his big black beard was matted wet and dripping.

His eyes shined bright within the dark rings from unmistakable exhaustion, but when he spied Larry standing there, his face fell, shaped to sadness and disappointment. He shook his head, his cheeks quivering, as he descended the last stairs. "Have you word?" he asked.

The desperation in the man's voice was genuine, confusing Larry. His distress was either the performance of a great betrayer or the honest bearing of an open wound.

"Did he send you word?" the Judge asked again, approaching without fear.

"Sven?" asked Larry, and to say the name was to feel the full weight of the Judge's anxiety and the overwhelming gravity of Larry's own fear. "No."

"Christ," said the Judge, his melancholy now overwhelming him. "Jesus Christ, Mr. Cornish. I am...I am sorry."

All the anger and self-apportioned malice Larry had built within himself, readying for this moment, vanished. It was perhaps the redness of the Judge's eyes and the weariness in his voice that proved true the man's distress. Something had happened to Sven, but this man had not been the cause.

"Judge?" said Mr. Priest.

He gave a sound of half-surprise. "No," he said. "No, it's alright, Jacob. I am at Mr. Cornish's full disposal and..." He looked deep into Larry's eyes—and in those eyes the gunfighter saw the weight of a thousand sleepless nights, a thousand nightmares, living behind their color—and placed the full weight of his hand on Larry's shoulder, as if they had known one another for years. "And...at his mercy," he said. "Please, come with me. We have much to discuss."

Inside room 1204, a spacious suite with a sitting room partitioned from the bedroom, was a slender man dressed in a brown twill suit. He sat upon a small couch with one leg crossed over the other, his stormy green eyes rimmed in golden spectacles. His hair was stringy and brown, like moss clinging to the stone of his alabaster face. Through the open cut of the doorway leading to the bedroom, a Black woman with a high brow, her face tired and shining from being freshly washed, appraised Larry as he entered.

"This is Mr. Larry Cornish," said the Judge, settling into a wooden desk chair opposite the couch. "He is Sven's companion and has come to us with questions, no doubt. Mr. Cornish, may I introduce my friends and agents, Professor Robert Bass and Sarah Lockhart."

They nodded, gave simple pleasantries.

Larry said nothing, but nodded, eyeing both of them hard.

"I will give you the long answer to your questions, should you require it, Cornish," said the Judge, slowly swiping his smoking pipe from the desk. "But this is as short as I can make it: my business is a bloody one, involving powers both mundane and strange. Sven was helping us track one of the stranger and more brutal actors within this hidden war in which we are engaged, when an object I do not understand was used to seize his mind. Possessed, he acted against us, and we were forced to run in fear of death at his capable hand. We fled both your husband and the forces of our enemy: a woman known as the Baroness who has cut a red line along the entirety of the Eastern Seaboard. She is the one who took your husband captive and possesses the object which bewitched his mind.

"We followed her, refusing to engage for lack of firepower but not wanting to abandon your man to her cruel whims. We know that she is here in Charleston, for she travels by way of a personal steam train, the *Hephaestus*. It remains at the station, and Professor Bass believes she has taken up residence somewhere among the still standing plantation homes just outside Charleston proper."

"That is my theory, yes," said the Professor, his voice airy, electric. "Her forces number too many to simply hotel them, and her purposes are too clandestine to trust to a public space. But there are many estates to check, and none of our investigations have yielded a result yet."

"There's also the fact that we are only a force of three," said the Judge. "I have wired other agents I trust in matters of martial purpose but have not heard back, which swells my worries about their own lives and missions. So, I hope you will see, Mr. Cornish, and believe, that while you would be right to question how Sven came to be kidnapped, I am at fault, but I am not to blame."

"I will join you," said Larry.

Ellison's bald head near wrinkled to the pate of his skull in surprise. "I cannot afford your gun. Your guild will never allow—"

"I am your fourth, no longer the Nine."

"You…quit?" asked the Judge.

"Of course he did," said Lockhart. "There was no choice but to leave that for this, was there, Mr. Cornish."

"No," said Larry.

The woman was grinning, understanding.

"I admit, you are a welcome aid to our cause," said the Judge. "I simply hope that the events to come will not wager too high a price, as recent events have already asked a great deal."

Larry regarded him and, having learned from the love of his life, spoke as Sven would have. "I am a gunfighter, Ellison—half gambler, half artist, and all competitor. The marketplace of time has set a price on my husband's life, and I will pay it. I will pay it today. In this place. I will ply my trade, and my vengeance will fetch a great premium here."

Just outside the room, racing feet clomped up the stairwell and stopped at the door behind Larry. "Mr. Judge," Tommy cried from the hallway, quickly followed by the little hammering of his fist on the door. "Mr. Judge!"

Larry looked to Ellison. "Another agent of yours?"

"Among many in training, though there are few younger or more eager than he." The Judge nodded at the door. "If you would?"

Larry swung the door open to let the boy in.

"Mr. Judge," said Tommy, breathless and hurried. "Andy seen that coach you asked us to watch for. He seen it rolling out of town."

"And did he follow?" asked the Judge, his eyes flashing with fresh energy.

"Yeah, far away, just like you said."

"Good. And?"

Tommy swallowed hard. "They was some lady they was driving. Fancy lady. Two men with her. Both armed to the teeth. Rough looking."

The Judge set his big hands on the boy's shoulders, careful, almost parental. "And where did they take her?"

"Andy followed 'em, Mr. Judge. Followed 'em all the way to the junction cutoff of Solomon Hall, which ain't nobody worked that place since after the war. We all thought it was abandoned. Used to throw rocks through the windows, Andy and me."

"Did he see anything else. Maybe how many men?"

"Lots of men, too many for the house. They have a little camp just behind the big house. Couple of coaches. Andy didn't get too close though, like you said. But there was lots of 'em. Holding rifles like they was on guard."

Judge Ellison flared his nostrils, taking in a deep breath, and the weariness of his face was burned away by the fire set alight in his eyes. He set those eyes on Larry Cornish. "Tonight. Under cover of dark. The grounds of Solomon Hall will see the restoration of your union, Mr. Cornish, or the hellfire of revenge.

SOLOMON HALL
CHARLESTON, SOUTH CAROLINA
9:45 P.M.
APRIL 1, 1866

Inside of Sven Erickson there was a secret place. From time to time, depending upon his mood or locale, what he saw, or what he smelled or heard, there would morph. Sometimes it was the lush memory of a hotel room; other times, a rolling spring prairie that he'd never seen but only imagined. It existed in a realm higher than his reason, beyond his intellect, and yet buried far below the deepest reaches of his heart. For near all the adult years of his life, he had used the solitude of that space to hone his martial skill to its sharpest edge. No matter who was the challenger or the challenged, no matter whether it was a ceremonial duel or an informal skirmish, it was access to this hidden place which gave him his advantage.

It was the key to his superiority with a gun. Sinking into that place settled the nerves and slowed his heart's fluttering beat to a steady drum ahead of the twenty-fifth step and the draw. It provided him focus, swiftness, accuracy, and ultimate solitude. Unshareable, he'd thought.

Until a year ago.

Until he'd met Larry Cornish.

"Again," came the voice of the Baroness.

And Sven, tied standing to a high bedpost, closed his eyes and sank deep into the secret space before the rending lash found once again the tatters of his back. The metal hooks sank into his flesh, striking like battering rams against the stone walls of his secret place, ripping and tearing as they were swiftly drawn back.

"Hmm," the Baroness sounded, disappointed. "Again, Roderrick."

In the distance between the whip cutting through the arc of time, Sven sheltered himself in the thought of Larry Cornish standing before the hotel door, ready to leave for Natchez. The man looking handsome, hawkish, calm-eyed, introspective. And in the half-second whirl of the whipcord sounding its collection of power, he remembered the music of Larry's voice. The touch of the sheets they had only the night before shared. The cool wind running its fingertips along their naked bodies. All that had led them to that sacred moment of goodbye.

The whip struck again, down his spine, raking tissue to blood.

The loss of flesh was nothing in the face of that mortal memory, but the impact once again shook the walls guarding the confidence and permanence of the man.

"What a specimen," said the Baroness. "What endurance for hardship."

Slathered in sweat and diminished of all worldly power to affect his situation, Sven closed his eyes and mouthed the words, "I love you, Larry."

The whip gathered speed once again, and he grit his teeth, readying for the strike.

"Heel," said the Baroness.

No strike, no fresh pain to guard against.

"Good boy, Roderick. You may go," she spoke, a hunter commanding a hound.

Feet shuffled. A door opened. Closed.

There was an empty space, heavy silence. Then what sounded like glass sliding upon wood. The noise of someone swallowing. The Baroness was drinking. Just sitting there, admiring at the ruin of him. Likely smiling.

Sven was so tired, and he was now back in the moment, overwhelmed by the fires of exhaustion and pain, unable to once again seek out that secret place.

"What is a man, but this," she said, considering, and took a deep breath. "This is you, all of you, reduced to your most basic element: constitution. Nature gives you this great gift—this strength—and look how you cling to it, like all the rest. You refuse to cry out though your eyes are wet with tears. You say nothing, holding all your injury inside. All because your pride tells you, 'Do not give this woman the satisfaction of your pain.'" And she laughed. "More's the pity for this, the base state of a man."

Sven said nothing.

There was the creak of a chair, and then the light footfalls of the Baroness's feet upon the wooden floor. "And it is beautiful, Sven Erickson," she said, placing the flat of her palm against the open wounds perforating his shoulder blade. Blinding pain shot down his spine, his hips, all the way to his feet, bound tight. "The blood." Pressing hard, she slid her hand across his back, rolling him open like a scroll. "The red of it. The *wetness*. The life of you so easily flows, given over to me."

And Sven cried out, more animal than man.

"How much do you think I should take?" she said, pinching a ribbon of skin and pulling so that it began to tear away. "A sliver here. Or perhaps I will simply allow my memory to photograph the little red streams, the bruises in blue, all of you made a great purple welt. And what a picture you are." She clicked her tongue. "Men like you often take this moment to curse or damn, but not you. You remain quiet in pride... or"—and she leaned close, so close he felt the heat of her breath on his ear—"hope. You're holding on to something. Is it the dream of the One Pin? Is it ambition that gives you your buoyancy?" She let out a low hum. "No. No, it can't be that. You men love your games, but you die *in* those games, not for them. No, you're remaining strong because of *someone*. I can see the life of your love as clearly as I can scent the iron in your blood. Tell me the name."

Sven took a deep breath, his swollen lips aching, as he said, "We do not say the name."

At that, the Baroness howled with glee. "Oh my, are you a joy, right down to the nub." And suddenly more pain, white hot, thrust into his flesh as the Baroness made knives of her fingers, thrusting them into the riven flesh.

Again he cried out, trying to pull away, though he was held fast.

"Tell me," she said, pressing her full weight into the violating hand, "the name."

A portion of his mind yearned to give over that which she asked for. His reason begged the secret place within his heart to open the fortifications and yield. Saying the name would bring relief, logic pleaded. Giving her what she wanted would mean nothing if it meant death. But the competitor stood a colossus against the voice of reason. "My name is Sven Erickson," he said, voice thrown to a fever pitch. "I am the Silver Pin Eleven."

Harder the Baroness shoved, deeper her fingers penetrated into the walls of his brawn. "Gunfighter through and through," she said, rapturous. "I know. Let us have a duel. That is what you do, yes?" And, as if suddenly taken by a mania, she slid he fingers free. She came around him, spinning on bare feet, his blood painting her alabaster skin from tiptoe to ankle. With every step, she left a little wet footprint—a ballerina dancing a trail of gore. A production for an audience of two, for Sven to watch and the Baroness to enjoy. Twirling, feet padding lightly across wooden slats, she approached a small hutch. Stopped. Then rested an index finger on her lips and turned, looking back at him as if she were about to reveal a secret. "What," she asked in a mocking tone, "have I found?"

The hutch groaned open, the hinges begging for oil. She reached a bloody hand into the darkness and, from that unseeable place, produced a revolver. Sven's revolver. It was much too large for her slender fingers, but when she gripped it, the strength in her hand could not be denied. "Tell me how you do it," she said, her focus set fully on the killing device. "Tell me how you challenge each other."

Sven said nothing. Gave nothing.

The Baroness drew the hammer of the revolver back. Licked her lips at the cocking sound. "It's heavy," she said. "My guess is that the life is heavy also, that of a gunfighter. The yoke of vanity and pride you must wear. To think"—she looked to the ceiling and into some grand vision she was creating—"no, to *know* that you are the very best at your trade while surrounded by twenty-four others who believe the same of themselves. You, Sven, you must live in a reality that attests your superiority, while all the others are simply dreamers." She squatted before him, becoming pure shadow as she was silhouetted by the light of the fire in the hearth behind her. "In this way, you and I are the same. I know I am superior. Designed for a grand purpose. And with sacrifice, Sven Erickson, I will change the world in a way you and this," she said, pressing the open barrel of the revolver against his head, "could never do."

Sven flattened himself upright against the post, slaked with sweat and breathing ragged. "We invoke challenge. Make clear our intent to duel. Call out our silver-pinned opponent and give them an opportunity to yield." The end of the barrel was cool, the little zero shape a small relief against his hot skin.

"Challenge me, gunfighter," said the Baroness.

"I challenge you," said Sven, his neck aching from holding his head upright.

"No. In your fashion." She slapped him lightly with her free hand, more mockery. "The fancy way you all do."

Sven shook his head, cast his gaze upon the floor. Blood ran down his back, buttocks, thighs, dripping. His every breath a struggle, his every want to die. But then he found at the center of himself, in that secret place, a memory. He remembered the man that he loved. He remembered Larry Cornish. And in the imagined eyes of his lover, his heart ignited, and the power of that vision, the clarity of it, was to know indomitability. Staring into that unreal, secret arena within himself, the gunfighter found truth and will, strength and illumination. To find the face of Larry in the midnight of that desperate hour was to discover fire for the second time.

He raised his eyes again, hardening them on the shadowed face of the Baroness. "My name is Sven Erickson. I am the Eleven. And I come to you now, Baroness, outside of the rank and rule of my association, and hereby challenge you to a contest of the gun. Lash me. Torture me. You will never break me. And should you kill me, know that the agent of my revenge will hunt you. A man greater than I will become a pestilence unto you and all your people. His name is Larry Cornish, and neither you nor your master will survive the test of war he will put upon you." Then, strong as he had ever been, he said, "Yield or die. The choice is yours."

There was a long, drawn-out silence, and in those moments his gaze never wavered.

The Baroness giggled. "You're something, you know that? I yield," she said playfully. "I yield." The pressure from the gun barrel eased for a moment, then pressed hard, the little circle of steel mashing so fiercely into his flesh it might slice him open. "Or maybe…I don't, Sven. Maybe I should blow your brains all over this room, wait for your revenger, and make him lick the floor clean. Like a good hound lapping up his master's spilled stew."

Done with this woman's gleeful bullshit and threats, he stretched out his neck, sinking the barrel deep enough to draw blood. "Do it," he said. "It'll save me the fucking headache of listening to you talk."

She laughed a hum. "Bold and fearless. It has been a pleasure to watch you bleed, gunfighter. A greater pleasure to know the name of he whom you love best. This Larry Cornish, he will come to avenge you because your hearts are intertwined. The stone which entranced you has a thirst for such things. Passion. Joy. Love. It drinks them all. Tonight, it will drink from–

There came a knock at the door, gentle, almost unassuming.

"*What is it?*" the Baroness screamed, her mania returning at the interruption.

"Baroness…" The man's voice was muffled, filled with worry. "She's here."

The Baroness inhaled sharply, eyes wide, and the gun fell away. Unmistakable, it was the surprise of joy. "Do you hear?" she asked Sven in a near-whisper. "You have no idea how fortunate you are, Eleven. You'll suffer me a bit longer as I transform you. A witness glorified to participant." She drew away, saying, "Roderick, get Smith and Brown. The three of you will dress Mr. Erickson and see him to the library."

"Yes, Baroness."

"And get the doctor, too, I suppose," she said over the sound of her hurried steps. "She'll want to see."

CHAPTER SIXTEEN

En Route to Solomon Hall
Charleston, South Carolina
11:25 p.m.
April 1, 1866

Their chances made best under the cover of darkness, Larry Cornish led the other riders through the night—a vanguard spear tip in a black suit. The moon, waning gibbous and bloody as an open wound, threw its color upon the world, staining the winding cobblestone streets, the dusty saloons and taverns, and the shrimp boats swaying in the Stono, making red the night. That light carmine.

He trotted Heartbeat along the humidity slicked streets of Charleston, carrying within him all the rage a man might bear. In one hand, the reins of Midnight were clinched in a fistful of hope. Hope that the horse would be needed and would soon feel the weight of his rider once again. As they passed through the mostly empty moon-lighted town, Larry centered himself, barely feeling the gait of the horse, knowing full well that tonight would prove the fulcrum of his life. Perhaps its end. Sven alive meant a harrowing battle to see him saved. Sven dead would mean cataclysm for those who had seen it done.

From behind him, the leader and agents of the Peregrine Estate spoke hurriedly, their voices too soft to make out all of it. Bass sounded like he was asking questions. Lockhart snapped back something, and the Judge ended the discussion, silencing their talk with the only clear portion, "...because a man doesn't choose the love, the love chooses him."

It was true, Larry knew. And it struck him in that moment, riding through the black shadows of the reddened town, that though he'd never been searching for the love of anyone or love for its own sake, love had found him anyway. Like the tireless sun striving each morning to crest over the gray hills of life indeterminate, Sven Erickson's love had shone with a light so bright and clear that Larry's faded world immediately burst into magnificent color. And it was strange, he thought, on this ride to the place where all things might end, that he fell not into his pit of cold calculation but into the hot, burning memories of first sight, first touch, first kiss. All the strength living within Sven's hands and arms and shoulders, the scent of his tobacco, the music of his laugh. Anyone who caught sight of him passing by on this night might first grow anxious at the sight of the silver pin on his vest, only to be more deeply vexed by the width of the grin on his face. And so, like Death smiling all the way to the funeral plot, Larry Cornish remembered.

When they were far enough outside of town that galloping would no longer draw attention, Larry squeezed Heartbeat and gave Midnight a little more slack. And the riders four raced over bridges and the ebbing stony streets unto trails which silently observed them gliding like spears cast into the night. The Peregrine folk came alongside Larry, masoning a rushing wall of righteous intent. Closest to Larry, Judge Ellison rode as if born anew, all his age cast aside by the wind running through his beard and the ancient fire of belief in his eyes. Sarah Lockhart rode with a smile shining scarlet in the red moonlight, her open cavalry vest snapping in the wind. Further down the line was Professor Bass, posted in the English style, tall and lean and stormy-eyed, ready to strike.

At a fork, the riders curved eastward. The thunderous sound of their mounts' hooves chopped through a slash of high growth made black by the shadows of oak trees who, given ten-thousand years of unimpeached growth, could never hope to touch the impossible canopy height of the will of force within Larry. Never had his life's direction been more clearly known. Never had his want to be the One pin touched this topmost place. He had found a meaning greater than gainful competition, a purpose higher than being the best at a fearsome skill. It had previously empowered him, had given him the capacity to wager life and death on the bleeding edge of a split-second, but now, charging alongside strangers upon a landscape unknown to him, Larry Cornish all at once found himself.

Became who he was meant to be.

A man who was never destined to be the greatest living gunfighter the world over, but rather a man who was willing to destroy those who dared threaten or maim or kill Sven Erickson, or the world in which he resided. The One pin would never belong to him, but Sven Erickson did. And that settled all competitions living within Larry Cornish for all the rest of time.

Another forking path, and Larry leaned eastward, his heart set on fire, though unburning. He glanced back to see the Judge, his smiling shootist, and the brazen academic riding hard at his heels. There in the distance, set between a colonnade of moonlight reddened maples running a mile, maybe more, was the ancient, white, and gloomy Solomon Hall. The maples shivered in the spring night wind, like ten-thousand bloody hands urging the riders to go no further.

"Kick for it!" howled the Judge, and with a sudden burst of speed his black mare lifted her neck but briefly, then lanced it forward, back and forth, carrying the barrel-like man as if he weighed little more than a sack of grain. Sarah brought to bear her gelding's full power, and so too the Professor, who rode so tall, so erect, hips moving in time with the powerful beast beneath him. And the riders of the Peregrine Estate drew alongside Larry, riding with fury in their eyes and anticipation writ upon their faces, their clothes near raveled to tatters in the blowing wind, floating in their speed. But he could not be overtaken.

But Larry Cornish could not be overtaken.Larry spied three men upon the balustraded porch of Solomon Hall, now perhaps two to three-hundred yards off. Two had set flatted hands to their foreheads, trying to peer into the darkness at the rushing thunder of horses they undoubtedly heard. The other man, standing upon the third-story balcony, revealed himself by sign of the moonlight flash, long and silver, against the telescopic sight of a rifleman lookout.

There was little time to choose. Larry wasted none of it. He released Midnight's reins and slowed only a little, then slapped the passing gelding on the rump, sending the horse straight ahead. Then, he leaned right, spraying Heartbeat's trajectory north, off the trail path that led to the dreary plantation home. If the rifleman kept his gaze within the scope's tunnel, he would spy riderless Midnight, giving Larry enough time to approach.

Twenty yards gained.

The Peregrine Trio followed Midnight, rushing unto Solomon Hall.

Thirty would have to do.

Larry brought Heartbeat to full stop, turning him broadside while sliding himself into full dismount. He reached into the buckskin sheath set along Heartbeat's pulsing ribs, gripped the polished wood stock, and produced his long gun —a Winchester '66. And with calm breath and cool, quick hand, he flipped up the Vernier sight and slid the barrel to rest upon the saddle. With keen vision sliding like thread through the eye of a sewing needle, Larry sighted the lookout.

One heartbeat. Two. Three.

One breath. The second breath held.

One slow draw on the trigger, and the windswept night awoke to the sound of thunder.

The lookout, staring down the silvering steel of his telescopic sight, suddenly blossomed at the skull, falling away in the red mist of all he would never be. Then quickly, back in the saddle and gun hidden away once again, Larry wheeled Heartbeat around. Unfettering the steed from all restraint, they slashed through the colonnade of maples to once again gallop upon the dark, powdery road running uninterrupted toward white-faced Solomon Hall. Before him, flashes of gunfire sparked, marking the air like turgid serpents of gunpowder smoke. The Judge was shouting and cursing, then, upon striking one of the Society gunmen, he bellowed a laugh wild and terrible. Sarah had dismounted and taken cover behind one of the sentinel trees, its dark bark shorn away in sections from the spray of enemy fire.

Larry rode, chewing up the distance between himself and the looming plantation.

Sarah, spinning out of cover, aimed and fired and missed, splintering white-washed wood from the house's double-doored frame. The final Society man thought to retreat, turning to rush inside, but she brought her revolver close to her side, fanning the hammer with a practiced motion which would have been the envy of near all the twenty-five Silver Pins. Three rounds struck the fleeing man, striping him red at hip and spine and shoulder. He fell, arms outstretched.

"We've got them on the run," cried Sarah, reloading as she looked up toward Larry.

Bass turned his gelding, gliding the aim of

his pistol to search for any sign of enemy from the balcony decks. "It's best to weigh the enemy more mighty than he seems," he said, dismounting. He slapped his horse on the rear, sending it to flee back the way they had come. "Anyone hit?"

As they assessed themselves for unnoticed wounds, Larry passed by, hearing only the sound of their words and none of their meaning. He stepped upon the porch, collected two pistols from the fallen gunmen, and headed for the door, fully armed and fearless of whatever wait for him within.

"Cornish!" the Judge yelled.

Larry stopped but did not turn.

"This is how we lost your man," he said. "It's a foolish mistake I will not allow a second time. Do not go in alone. They'll be holed up and may have Sven hostage."

Larry glanced over his shoulder, one eye appraising the Judge as he approached.

"Hear me," the Judge said, red faced. "If not for my sake, for Sven's. If they see they have no way out and you're not to be reasoned with, they'll slaughter him without hesitation."

Larry, his furious rage swirling with cyclone power, took a deep breath, trying to calm himself. "Plan?"

"Always. Now, without knowing your full capability I must ask, and I mean no offense: Do you think you can assault the auxiliary guard? They've heard the gunshots and will be rousing from their beds as we speak. Can take them yourself?"

Larry did not hesitate. "I am the fastest gun in the world tonight, Judge Ellison," he said, cold and mean, believing every single word of it. "There is nothing I cannot take that I *decide* to take."

CHAPTER SEVENTEEN

WITHIN SOLOMON HALL
CHARLESTON, SOUTH CAROLINA
11:25 P.M.
APRIL 1, 1866

R acked with pain, time having little meaning, Sven all at once found himself unlashed from the post. He was taken by many hands and made to stand as they dressed him in pants and shirt. With his boots and gun left in the room, and he was forced to shuffle barefoot through the plantation house halls, falling to his knees many times. He suffered his captors' kicks and japes, and they gave no assistance when he was required to rise.

"Not so fucking scary without that gun, are you, *Silver Pin*," one man said. Then spat in Sven's eyes. The man smiled, drew close. "Not so—"

Sven headbutted the man in the face. There

was a satisfying crunch, and the man's blood splashed hot across Sven's forehead. That warranted him a good beating, which he took helplessly as the men rained down blows upon his lacerated back and ribs. One boot caught Sven flush on the jaw, causing his teeth to bite a hunk out of his tongue.

"He got you good, Brown," said another man.

"Yeah. We'll see if he thinks it was worth it after I get me one of those fingers. Mr. Smith," he said, his voice was full of venom. There came the sound of metal sliding clear of leather, something sharp and long. "Hold him fast."

Vision blurred, fatigue and injury stealing all his great strength, Sven was yanked to his feet. Someone took him by the wrist and mashed his palm flat against the wall. The blade moved into view, coming to rest just above his index finger. With a single stroke of that knife, all of Sven's great prowess and skill would be eliminated.

He would not allow these men to steal that from him. Drawing upon all his reserves, he threw an uppercut with his left hand, smashing Brown under the chin. At the connection of that blow, a raging pulse of energy surged within him, and a momentary hope that if he were to kill these men barehanded, he could still retrieve his gun—it was within walking distance. He lashed out, spinning hard to pull free of his captor's grip. Once free, he grabbed a man by the collar and again crashed his forehead into the man's face.

Two men felled, he turned to find the third.

But the third man found Sven first.

Something cold and hard bit deeply into his thigh. Sven buckled, falling to the ground and clutching his leg. His advantage vanished as swiftly as it had arrived. As each of the three captors recovered, they once again began putting the boots to Sven, until even his unassailable pride was forced into docility. Unable to rise, he was then dragged by his heels down a flight of steps, tatters of his flesh peeling back beneath his shirt, caught by the unforgiving runner carpet of the stairs. He was pulled along the wooden floorboards until the blurry ceiling finally came to stop, and a woman cried out.

"My god," she said. "What is this, Gwenny? Who is—"

The Baroness shushed gently. "Hush, my love. This man is a part of the grand design. His life is forfeit. He is a killer, plain and simple. A gunhand hired to kill me and my men. And make no mistake, if he were armed again, he would happily finish the mission he was sent to accomplish."

"I…" The woman seemed flustered. "I don't understand. I have come to you as asked, but this, Gwenny... this is nothing like what you wrote."

Unsure if he could do any more than breathe, Sven tried to roll over. He made it to his side and rested upon one shoulder. Into his vision came the Baroness, and the woman standing next to her. She looked so young, he thought. So young in that white dress of hers, her black curls shining like silk in the lamplight. They were in some kind of ballroom with polished wooden floors and a great hearth. A grand piano stood in the corner near a small table, and there upon it, a sphere of dark green stone.

"Do you love me, Claramay?" asked the Baroness.

"What?" The woman sounded insulted. "After all you have put me through, I come to this place at your behest, and you dare ask me such a question? I've come, Gwen. I've raced to forgive you, and you greet me in this strange place with a beaten man and tell me stories of—"

"Answer," commanded the Baroness. She placed a gloved hand upon Claramay's cheek. "Do you love me?"

Claramay leaned into the touch, her eyes closing at its gentle power.

"Say you love me." The Baroness stroked her lover's face.

"I—" The word was little more than a breath. "I do."

"I know," said the Baroness. "And I know. And I you, sweet spring flower. You own the whole of my heart. You have for all the days since the first of our meeting and for all the rest of my life. I belong to you, as you belong to me."

Soothed, the woman rested her fingers over the gloved hand set upon her face. "I know," she said. "And I know."

"Will you help me, Claramay? As only you can?"

"Yes," she said, then breathed deep, letting out as a sigh.

"Good girl, my love. Now, come and see." The Baroness glided her hand from cheek to the small of Claramay's back, and then guided her toward the depth of the room, toward the table with the emerald stone set upon it.

"No," said Sven, knowing the full intent of the Baroness's plan.

I am designed for a grand purpose, she had said to him. *And with sacrifice, Sven Erickson, I will change the world…*

"No," he said again, louder. "Run."

"Shut the fuck up," said Brown, and kicked Sven so hard in the ribs it crushed all the wind from his lungs.

"Ignore the barking hound, my heart," said

the Baroness. "And look and see: the wedding gift I have fashioned for you."

"A stone?" asked Claramay, bewildered and unsure.

"No, no, no," said the Baroness. "Your gift is here, my love, set within the silks."

Sven tried to speak a warning, but no words came. Every breath was a dagger to his lungs.

From the table, Claramay lifted the silk-wrapped object. "It's heavy," she said, pleased by the weight of the gift. "Shall I guess before I unwrap it?"

The Baroness's smile slowly widened. "If it pleases you."

"It's thick here, like a handle." The white of her dress shimmered gossamer in the hearth-light. "But it thins toward the—ow!" She dropped the gift, and a slender knife spilled out of the colorful silks and clattered on the floor..

"Oh, love," said the Baroness. "Careful. Are you hurt?"

"I cut my hand. I'm bleeding!" Claramay, so distressed and yet so soothed by the Baroness's careful way, she could not see. Could not know what was happening.

There came a strange noise. A low hum. Growing melodic. Ancient and unknowable.

The mine, thought Sven, still immobile. *The music from the mine.*

"We have to be careful, my love. My heart

and spring flower," said the Baroness, leaning down to pick up the fallen dagger. "Now," she said, lifting the blade so that the little spray of red upon the silver steel caught the light. Not the light of the hearth, but from another source. The two women, one the color of the purest fallen snow and the other black as the void of space, were illuminated in a pale green light. "Look and see, Claramay. Listen and hear."

The sound of voices reached from beyond any knowable place, filled the air, issued from the throats of invisible and indivisible choir. Angels or demons they might have been, or perhaps something more terrible than both. The voices filled the room with a song composed for the sake of...not beauty or fellowship or love... though they counterfeited the sound.

Oppression, thought Sven. And the song reached within him once again, as it had done in the mine. Touched the center of him and weighed the very soul inside him. And then, finding him no longer capable, no longer a weapon to be used in his state of brokenness, the hand of the dark hymn receded. It had appraised the gunfighter and found him unworthy of its power.

"What is happening?" cried Claramay, wholly terrified. "Gwenny, protect me." And for want of comfort and care, she reached for the woman who had called her to Solomon Hall.

The Baroness drew back her arm and, with a rapturous smile upon her dark lips, thrust the length of the blade so deep into Claramay that it slid cleanly through her ribs out the other side, tattering her white dress to red. "Ascension," was all she said.

Claramay inhaled, her eyes widening with the shock of betrayal. And she gripped the Baroness at the shoulders, as if trying to hold herself upright.

The Baroness drew Claramay into a tight embrace, holding the woman fast even as her arm became a furious piston. "I love you for this," she said, the knife sliding in and out of Claramay in quick, smooth strokes. "More than you can know. More than you can know." The blade sprayed blood upon them both with each successive plunge. "More than you can ever know."

Ragged little breaths fluttered like dying butterflies from Claramay's paling lips as she fell to her knees, clutching at her betrayer with confusion in her eyes.

All through the woman's dying, the Baroness never ceased in her relentless effort to drive all the life from the living. "I love you. I love you. I love you," over and over she spoke. And over her words the great sound of the song rose once again, the green stone pulsing with singular strangeness, where it bathed the room in its sickly incandescent light.

Until the end of his days, Sven Erickson would remember the sight of the green light, its irrepressible song, and how the blood of Claramay began to rise from the mutilated body, the dress it wore, and the ground it lay upon. And he would remember the wild eyes of the Baroness, the red wetness slowly drawn from her gloves, and the blood. The goddamn blood floating toward the toward the stone, and the way in which it drank the air dry.

The song too terrible to endure, the pain too mighty to overtake, Sven resigned himself to die. And, closing his eyes and letting go of all his earthly hopes, he sank within himself and found the secret venue within his heart where he had given Larry Cornish a home. So clear did that man come into view that Sven was over-whelmed. Tears filled his eyes. With those tears, Sven spoke the words he knew would be his last, unheard by the man to whom they were directed.

"I love you, Nine," he said.

Then, as he readied himself to say his lover's name one last time, a gunshot cracked the air. Its repeat sounded in time with the nightmare song spilling from the emerald stone. Sven opened his eyes to see every Prometheus Society member in the room turn shocked gazes toward the westward windows.

More gunfire sounded—a wild volley just outside.

"The Judge!" howled the Baroness. "The goddamn Judge and Bass and Lockhart. Rouse the rest of the men. Kill them!"

Brown peered out the window and shook his head. "I count four."

The Baroness looked at Sven, her eyes wide.

Broken and slashed all over, Sven nodded and smiled. "You're one dead bitch," he said.

"We'll see who dies tonight." And she came at him in a rush, knife lifted.

The windows exploded with gunfire, and Brown's head burst open, his brains splattering the ground as he fell. Smith cried out, sprawling to his belly.

And from out of the night, in momentary silence fallen upon Solomon Hall, there came a bold voice. The voice of Hezekiah Ellison.

"Baroness!" He drew out the word long and threatening. "Does Sven Erickson live?"

"Damn you, Ellison," the Baroness called out, motioning to Smith to get his attention. "Erickson lives, but for how long, who can say?"

"It is good for you that he is alive. It allows me to address you with a choice. Surrender now and we will fire no more. You will stand trial before a jury of your peers for the crimes you have committed. Refuse, and I swear to god not a single soul you hold as an asset will leave this fucking house alive.”

“Now,” the Baroness commanded in a harsh whisper. “Smith, now! Round the back, take the rest of the men. Swing around and kill them all.”

“What’ll it be,” said Ellison. “The way of the law or the way of the gun?”

CHAPTER EIGHTEEN

SOLOMON HALL
CHARLESTON, SOUTH CAROLINA
12:27 A.M.
APRIL 2, 1866

"*Erickson lives*," the Baroness had proclaimed, and that proclamation did more than give Larry hope. The words changed him. They reshaped the anxiety and fear of arriving too late to save he who meant everything to him. The shrill voice of the Baroness, calling out from that shattered window within Solomon Hall, made over Larry Cornish, the Nine.

Though he bore not the pin, tonight he would be as fast as the One. As fast as any One Pin in the span of Guild history.

Around the corner of Solomon Hall, Larry walked alone. He stripped from his shoulders the black frock coat, dropping it among the moon-reddened maple leaves. It fell empty among the tree litter in the shape of half a man. He rolled his sleeves to cuffs, shoving them each to cinch high on his forearms. Boots crunching, spurs ringing with every step, he emptied himself of all caution and terror and worry of loss.

Tonight he would be fast. Accurate. Economic in every movement. Tonight, unlike all nights before in his life, he would be the most dangerous man alive.

He was the gunfighter who loved Sven Erickson, and he would transform himself.

Set within the lawn, fifteen yards and no more beyond the back porch of the plantation house, the shadows of soldiers rustled to arm themselves within nine lamplit canvas tents, many of them calling out "hurry!" or *goddamn* for getting in each other's way or failing to rouse at the call of battle. From out of the back of the house, a man burst from the doorway. He ran toward the camp and screaming, "Arm yourselves! We are under—"

Larry drew, fired.

The man fell to his belly, never to speak again.

Larry holstered the revolver and continued forward, never breaking stride.

"They firin' on us," screamed a man as he peeked out from the flap of his canvas tent, making the last mistake of his life.

Larry drew, fired again. The man's head

snapped back, spraying his blood and skull and brains upon the curve of the tent's canopy.

"Near the house!" said a woman, scrambling on all fours toward tree cover. "Just one! He's coming around the eastern side of the goddamn house!"

A pivot. An aim. The pull of a trigger. And the woman, struck in the side of the face, sprawled forth on limp arms, sliding to a stop amid the low-cut grass. She gazed blankly at the gunfighter, never to see again.

A trio of men poured out of a tent, one with no shirt, another with no boots, the third in long underwear, furiously scanning to find Larry Cornish stepping toward them with a smoking gun in his hand.

"There!" Shirtless announced.

The three men raised their pistols. Larry ducked, rolled to his left as the gunfire volley sailed wide, came up halfway, and settled on one knee as he fired once, twice, three times.

Shirtless lost an eye.

Bootless shivered, gut shot, and dropped his pistol as he fell to the ground.

The man in long underwear spun, clutching the bloom of red marking his heart.

"Shoot him, goddamn it!" a voice from somewhere in the darkness, too far beyond the tripod fires for Larry to spy a clear target. The blackness ignited with rifle shots, peppering the ground before him. He'd previously walked with sheer, undeniable purpose, but he now ran, tossing away the empty pistol. In his rush toward the protective row of maple trees, he drew a fresh revolver and blind-fired two rounds to cover his flight.

"It's one guy," a soldier called out. "One fucking guy."

"Don't let him get behind those trees, boys!"

Another salvo of fresh bullets whistled by as Larry rounded a maple, the bark splintering about his shoulders and face.

"We got him now! Form up on me. Everyone sighted on that tree."

Larry, back flattened against the maple, drew in his breath slowly. Though his shoulders were shaking, his hands remained steady.

"Where the fuck you goin', Jack?"

"We got him, captain. We can flush him out." The man's voice was high and tinny. "Hell, it's five to one—"

"Get your ass back here and shut the fuck up," commanded the captain. "Hey, over there!"

Larry broke open the pistol and replaced the two spent shells.

There came a moaning cry. "Captain, I'm hit."

"Jack, check on Tully," said the captain. "Hey, mister, you've killed six of my men—"

"Count it seven, boss," said Jack. "Tully's gutshot."

"Jack, don't say that to me," the voice whimpered. "Don't say that. I'm gonna be okay."

"You ain't, Tull. I'm awful sorry. It is mortal."

"That son of a bitch!" Tully's voice raised to a shrill pitch. "You goddamn son of a bitch. Who the fuck do you think you are?"

From within Solomon Hall, the sound of gunfire came.

Sven, thought Larry. *There was no time for this. No time for caution.*

"My name is Larry Cornish," he said. "Gunfighter and mercenary arm of the Peregrine Estate. You took my husband captive." He grit his teeth and summoned all of his courage and clarity of focus. "And I have come to take him back." He lengthened then squeezed tight his fingers around the butt of the revolver. "For he does not belong to you."

He ratchetted back the hammer, smooth and quick.

"He belongs to me."

Larry spun out of cover and saw all things clearly. In the moonlight glow of the midnight hour, five men came into view, guns in their hands, each in their own way masked in surprise. And there was no hesitation, no reservation; it was a moment of pure existence. All his motion aligned as a singular force hard-set on one shining purpose: to win. Not for money or pins or acclaim, but for the sake of a love that might endure this night and all other nights to come. He slapped the steel of the hammer in a fast one-two, spun back behind the tree, came around the other side fast as desperation might make a man, and clapped thunder three more times.

Larry had fired five shots.

Every one of them true.

He exhaled, looking over the camp slaughter as a man might appraise a stretch of land he once coveted but no longer wishes to buy.

"Larry!" the Judge called from within he house. "She's coming toward you!"

Larry whirled, gun rising to meet the darkened doorframe of the house. There was a little pop. A flash of light.

And he found himself falling, a burning pain suddenly manifesting within his chest. As if viewing from a remote distance, he watched the gun spill from his fingers and float through the air, drawn away as if by invisible string. The house, the gun, the fingers, all of it seemed so far, far away. He fell into the cool grass but felt none of the impact. In his ears there was yelling and screaming and gunfire then only the sound of his breathing. Each breath more labored than the one before.

"Sven," he said, gazing through the red

hands of the maple leaves into the blue, winking stars scattered across the night. And the darkness beyond their color. "Sven Erickson." His voice was soft and distant, longing for an ear.

Someone called his name.

The ground was more than cool now; it was cold. So cold it seemed to pull all the warmth from him, drinking deeply.

The swaying maple leaves grew blurry, melting to black. The darkness swallowed their color. Then it took the stars.

CHAPTER NINETEEN

THE HOUSE OF THE GUN
NEW ORLEANS, LOUISIANA
APRIL 17, 1866

New Orleans, unseasonably cool for an April day, opened its hospitable arms to a trio of riders making their way through her mostly empty streets. It was so quiet —its residents likely still sleeping off a drunk from the night before—that the sounds of the nature surrounding it spilled through the whole town. Cardinals sang their fierce love songs as they fluttered from oak branch to oak branch, willing to spar among the Spanish moss for the right to increase their progeny. Wind chimes caught the breeze. And the three men rode, adding the patient stride of their horses' hooves to the quiet splendor of the morning.

Judge Hezekiah Ellison was at the center of the trio, riding a big American Standard, gray and white with a braided mane and tail, regal as a king. "You two are sure, now?" he asked. "I cannot promise any better situation than the one we just survived."

Larry Cornish rode Heartbeat, slouched in the saddle, heavy bandages bracing his chest and ribs hidden beneath his twill shirt of green and gold. "Yes," was all he said.

"Larry and I are of one mind," said Sven Erickson, who rode tall despite the multitude of injuries plaguing him. He wore loose fitting clothing to spare his flesh but carried himself with the same confident pride and moxie displayed by the hopeful birds fluttering about the trees.

And for the first time in a long while, Hezekiah Ellison smiled. "Good," was all he said.

They made their way to the House of the Gun, where they were admitted entrance by the same guard Sven had threatened to kill on the night of the convocation.

"You planning on shooting your way out this time?" asked the guard, a smile on his young face.

"If I am," remarked Sven, "you'll be the first one to know."

"Or the last," said the guard, fearless in his gallows humor.

Up the wending pebbled path they went, the Judge leading the way. Under the fairytale-like arch of the House of the Gun once again, Larry and Sven laced their fingers together as they walked, their hopes bound up in the Judge's plan. There was risk involved, that was for certain, but no risk was too great when life together was the potential reward.

Boris, ancient and professional as ever, granted the trio entry and collected their pistols. Though he said nothing to the effect, the smile on his wrinkled face revealed his happiness to see the two gunfighters alive and together. The venerable custodian guided the men along the portrait hall, where dozens of painted eyes watched them go by. The Judge struck his pipe to life, never losing stride. Sven attempted to unclasp his hand from Larry's as they had always done, but Larry held fast, refusing to let go.

"Judge Hezekiah Ellison," said Boris, announcing the party before the three members of the Gunfighters Guild's governing body. "Sven Erickson, the Eleven. And Larry Cornish, unpinned."

Larry and Sven walked into the palatial drawing room before the three Golden Pins and presented themselves united, not as two men but as one.

Old Mute Cain stood near the French doors, his midnight skin made all the darker by the morning light behind him. Joshua Millsap, dressed in a gunmetal gray suit, was sitting next to radiant Belle Starr, who wore a silk dress the red of a poppy field, both holding steaming coffee cups.

"Welcome and welcome and welcome," said Belle Starr, her lips parting to reveal that carefree smile of hers. "Each of you deserve the word for yourself. Come and sit, especially you Judge Ellison, for I am greatly interested in the story you will tell. It no doubt involves you using your patron status to refuse my Silver Pins the opportunity to report back to us during these long anxious weeks."

Old Mute Cain walked, silently appraising all the way, and sat down on the empty leather chair next to Belle Starr.

The Judge, holding his pipe in one hand and gesturing performatively all through the story, told of all that had happened, and told it mostly true. He explained how, in her mad dash to escape with the strange stone, the Baroness had gotten the drop on Larry Cornish, and how the Peregrine Estate and Sven had rushed to Larry's aid rather than pursue the terror that had cut a red line all along the Eastern Seaboard.

"About the cost," said the Judge. "It seems that while I was accompanied by your two Silver Pins doing the work of my estate, my ranch boss was able to strike a considerable trade of beef with the Texas government. I have never been much a cattleman, and it seems in leaving others

I trust to run that operation, I struck it rich. Now, I have never been a lucky man…" He looked to Larry and Sven, then back to the Gold Pins. "But I have always been superstitious, and I find these two men as valuable to me as the lily of the valley was to the kings of old. A remedy to my otherwise infamous poor fortune. And so, with my wealth and my mission still unachieved, I will retain them in my employ."

"How long?" asked Millsap.

"A day, a year. I cannot say. What I can say is, until my work is accomplished. Which is another way of saying: indefinitely. Until all the world is set right or my coffers run dry. Selfishly, my hope resides with the former."

"Larry Cornish has renounced his pin," said Belle Starr, lifting an eyebrow. "He did so here, to me."

"I claimed retirement to one Gold Pin," said Larry Cornish. "Not all three."

Belle Starr's eyebrow cocked higher. "So you did, Mr. Cornish." Her grin was foxlike. "And that is the letter of the law with the Rule of Three."

"No rule or judgment," said Larry. "I will take back my pin. Reclaim the Nine. Sign on with Ellison."

"Well, therein lies the problem," she said. "You cannot reclaim the Nine. There have been three deaths in the last few months. Chelsea Vermillion the One. Calico Pip, Two. And just last week, Paul Moody, cleared of wrongdoing against Michael Horner for lack of evidence, killed the Seven, the poet gunfighter Amal Gladstone. All these duels have shuffled the pins, dear Larry. If you are to take back a pin, I'm afraid that puts you to the Six. And you, Sven Erickson, to the Eight. Still a gunfighter between you."

Sven reached into his pocket. "Heard about Moody killing Gladstone. Knowing that would advance the numbers, we went ahead and made stop in Alabama, and wouldn't you know it, I just happened to run into Pete Hammond." With a flick of his wrist, he tossed a silver pin bearing the number ten upon its face toward Joshua Millsap. The old gunfighter, fast as cat, snatched it out of the air and appraised it.

"So it seems you did, Mr. Erickson."

"Seven, you mean," said Sven. "Right next to the Six. Where I will remain."

Millsap ran his tongue over his teeth, frustrated. "You have set the odds in favor of freezing the game," he said. "Were it not for your patron employer, you could be compelled to draw down on one another, here and now, in the Silver Maple Wood."

"Fancy that," said the Judge. "What a joy it is to be a barrier for the sake of two players in the game I so heavily despise. But I will pay to blockade, Mr. Millsap. Your guild loves competition and hates to turn down a coin paid for the quickdraw skill you all dutifully worship. So you will take my money, and I will count it money well spent."

"You will give us letters of your mission's progress," said Belle Starr, rising to her feet. "Sending them regularly, along with chests filled with the color of your wealth."

"Silver and gold," said Judge Ellison.

Starr nodded and winked at the Seven and the Six. "For the Gold and Silver."

THE PEREGRINE ESTATE
ABILENE, TEXAS
MAY 29, 1866

Judge Hezekiah Ellison stood beneath the shadow of an old oak tree, dressed fine and proper in a black suit. The ancient oak stretched its limbs out toward the little river which ran beside it and would do so until the end of time. Before him, a collection of his agents stood in a staggered row, all dressed in their formal best. The falconer had called, summoning all his nearby birds that they might come together not for gloomy planning or desperate need of aid but for celebration. And with a high pride, he looked them over one by one.

There was the Professor Robert Bass with that devil-may-care smile resting beneath the open cap of a silver whiskey flask. Next to him, the aging Mary O'Shea, a remarkable woman of unremarkable feature, sheathed in buckskin leathers and bandoliered in knives. She was a veteran of the California Werewolf Campaign, soon to head to Chicago. Just behind her, the bright-eyed gambler Ashley Sutliff, who he'd soon send on another mission, asking for more though the man had already given so much. To his right, casting a shadow long as any man might at the three o'clock hour of a spring day, was his brother Ellery. Across a little gap, which would soon be used for procession, stood Gilbert Ptolemy and his young, adopted boy Carson. The two seemed a well-matched duo with their solemn expressions earned in shared tragedy, hats in their hands.

"Will it start soon?" asked the boy.

"All things in their time, son," said Ptolemy, a rare grin on his face.

"Never be afraid to wait, Carson," said Sarah Lockhart, who stood on the other side of the boy. Wearing a dress of gold and green, with her hair wild as a dandelion puff, she was a portrait of fierce beauty. Stooping, she looked deep into the boy's grass-green eyes and said, "Nothing good gets away." She then flicked her gaze to the boy's father, saying nothing with her words and every-thing with her stare.

Behind them all, standing the width of the

collective row away from each other, were the grooms. The reason for the celebration.

Sven Erickson, wearing a sharp suit of houndstooth navy, checkered in white, gazed longingly across the processional gap between himself and Larry Cornish. Larry, moderate in every measure, wore the black suit he'd donned to face Solomon Hall. He'd accented it with a scarlet silk puff tie set upon a long-sleeved white shirt, cuffed in the French style. Neither man wore a gun or silver pin. The springtime sun caught him at such a slant that the Judge may well have seen tears in his eyes.

The little crowd settled to full quiet.

The sounds of the river, for a moment, crowded over the grooms and witnesses and the officiant Judge, celebrants all.

The Judge began. "We are all come together for as grand a purpose as the world will allow. A celebration of one of the innumerable victories in love's long campaign to capture the hearts of all humankind. Here before us are now come Larry Joseph Cornish and Sven Erickson. I bid you now applaud these grooms as they approach to make vows and intertwine the fingers of their hearts, that they might hold tight forever to one another."

The agents of the Peregrine Estate began to clap.

Sarah set her fingers between her teeth,

whistling so loud it carried far beyond the ancient oak and the river, its elder.

Ellery drew his pistol to fire a celebratory shot in the air, but Ashley set a hand upon his brother's elbow and, shaking his head, said something which gave the younger, bigger Sutliff disappointed pause.

The two grooms stepped twenty-five paces apiece to meet in the middle of the narrow path that led to the Judge, ceremony, and the rest of their lives. They walked together, shoulder to shoulder, upon green grass and sprays of wild-flowers spanning near the whole spectrum of divinity's grand purpose of color.

To the end of his days, of all the things Judge Hezekiah Ellison accomplished by way of schemes and half-truths, valor and sacrifice, the joining of these hearts would mark more than the time. It would mark itself one of his highest honors.

The grooms took their place before the Judge and turned to face one another.

And there, upon the ground legally appor-tioned to Judge Ellison and set unto the labor of his estate's clandestine mission, standing within a bar of shadow made by the old oak tree against the hard Texas sunlight, Larry and Sven made their vows.

And kissed.

Kissed in sight of friends, all creation, and,
the Judge believed, smiling God above.

The End

About the Author

C.S. Humble is the award-winning American novelist of the Amid the Vastness of All Else Saga. He is also a screenplay and short story writer. He lives in East Texas.

A Note from Shortwave Publishing

Thank you for reading *Baroness of the Eastern Seaboard*! If you enjoyed this book, please consider writing a review. Reviews help readers find more titles they may enjoy, and that helps us continue to publish titles like this.

For more Shortwave titles, visit us online. . .

OUR WEBSITE
shortwavepublishing.com

SOCIAL MEDIA
@ShortwaveBooks

EMAIL US
contact@shortwavepublishing.com